Not without Reason and Other Stories

Rajee Seth is an acclaimed Hindi writer of fiction, poetry and criticism. Her works have been translated into almost all Indian languages as well as English. Among her most celebrated works is her translation into Hindi of Rilke's letters. She has received several awards, among them the First Tagore Literature Awards (2010), Hindi Academy Samman (1987), Bharatiya Bhasha Puraskar (1985), Rashtra Bhasha Gaurav Samman (2007). She was a Fellow at the Indian Institute of Advanced Study, Shimla. Seth lives and works in Delhi.

Raji Narasimhan writes fiction and criticism in English, and is also a well-known translator. Her novel, 'Forever Free', was on the English Literature course of IIT, Delhi, and was shortlisted for the Sahitya Akademi Award (1979–80). 'Sensibility Under Stress: Aspects of Indo-English Fiction' was recommended reading in English departments in Aligarh Muslim University and Utkal University, and was also shortlisted for the Sahitya Akademi Award (1976–77). Her translation of Maitreyi Pushpa's novel, 'Alma Kabutari' was shortlisted for the Crossword Translation Award in 2006–7. Narasimhan lives and works in Delhi.

Not without Reason and Other Stories

Rajee Seth

Translated from the Hindi by Raji Narasimhan

Orient BlackSwan

ORIENT BLACKSWAN PRIVATE LIMITED

Registered Office
3-6-752 Himayatnagar, Hyderabad 500 029 (A.P.), India
e-mail: centraloffice@orientblackswan.com

Other Offices
Bangalore, Bhopal, Bhubaneshwar, Chandigarh, Chennai,
Ernakulam, Guwahati, Hyderabad, Jaipur, Kolkata,
Lucknow, Mumbai, New Delhi, Noida, Patna

First Published 2012
Rajee Seth's stories in Hindi translated by Raji Narasimhan

ISBN 978 81 250 4512 0

Typeset in Bembo 11/14.6 by
Jojy Philip, New Delhi 110 015

Printed at
Aegean Offset Printers, Greater Noida

Published by
Orient Blackswan Private Limited
1/24 Asaf Ali Road, New Delhi 110 002
e-mail: delhi@orientblackswan.com

Contents

Introduction

The Many Faces of Pain

To call Rajee Seth a feminist writer would not be wrong. But it would be a half-truth. Many stories in this collection are stories about human failings, and human problems not centred on man-woman schisms or dichotomies, 'Wait, Intezaar Hussain', 'Yatra', 'My Option', for instance. Her aliveness to pain in human relations goes beyond gender-based perceptions to apprehending it as incumbent in life. There is no escape from pain, she says. And, more importantly, that pain is not always a synonym for unhappiness.

Stories such as the ones mentioned above are, however, obvious evidences of her trans-feminist disposition. The characters in them are men. It is so even in 'My Option', where Nilima, the narrator's sister, with her very feminine-seeming opposition to her husband's crude India-bashings, is not the initiating force of the story; it is her brother, the narrator, who performs that function. The interesting thing is that Seth's trans-feminism emerges from her woman-centred stories too. And this makes the latter more challenging, more connected to the basic proposition I make about her writing—that without damage to the feminist cause, her espousals mellow and expand to a philosophic awareness of pain as an intrinsic component of life, human or non-human.

There's no mincing of words, no soft-pedalling, in portraying the male atrocities dealt with in the story 'Not Without Reason' ('Akaaran to Nahee'). It is an open narration of the face-saving devices easily available to Sudhakar for making his wife the scapegoat for his sexual deficiency. The wife's rising sense of rebellion against these machinations of her husband is the parallel strand in the narrative. The parallel snaps, which is the point of climax in the story. The wife decides not to come back from her parents' where she is set to go.

She cuts loose, in other words. It seems like a classic, tit-for-tat, combative feminist ending.

But read the concluding lines again, and you sense what the author is saying without stating. 'With absolute clarity Deepali was seeing that like her sudden decision to go, the decision not to come back was also forming in her with swift, sure strides'.

That paragraph has a solid, concrete feel to it. Phrases like 'absolute clarity', and 'swift, sure strides', and Deepali's seeing the formation within her of her sudden decision to go make for an overall image composed of positives. And into this composition of positives is inserted the phrase, 'the decision not to come back'. It is terse and decisive enough of tone even if it is a negative. But it is without the firm, defined borders of the positive phrases. It brings in its wake the question of what next, raises the cloud of uncertainties that surround women taking decisions like Deepali's. And these uncertainties are voiced in the narrative all through. We see them in the monologues of Deepali, that, as said before, parallel the unfolding of the theme of the story, namely, the husband's impotence. From the backdrop of uncertainties a basic fact emerges: that Deepali is friendless, will probably remain so. There is no one speaking for her, no one taking her side. Her periodic visits to her parents' home are made only to 'unwind, be herself ... away from Hiro's (mother-in-law) nagging'. But will this relief her parents afford her stretch to their taking responsibility for her once more? Will her parents see her through the difficult transition period she will have to undergo to cope with single living? These issues are not taken up directly. But they loom over the body of the narrative.

The reality of intrinsic friendlessness emerges as an undercurrent in the dialogue between Deepali and Nisha, a neighbour. The whole scene is a cameo of the coded underhandedness of traditional behaviour that the parties concerned can decode at the slightest hint. The hint here is in three short sentences that Nisha speaks: 'Just came over to meet you. Who knows when we'll meet again. If we will at all'.

We can hear the words. They speak. They have a sound track away and apart from the voice of the speaker. We hear the heavy droop in the sentence, 'Who knows when we'll meet again'. We hear the conclusive helplessness and dead finality of the words, 'If we will at all'. The droop, helplessness and finality speak a language we know. And in a reflex action we move back to the source of the familiar inflections, till the English casing of the words dissolves and we hear the Hindi stored in the heart of the English. 'Jaane kab milen: mil bhi payenge kya pataa'.

Deepali catches on at once, what Nisha had caught on already, as soon as she heard that Deepali was going to her parents'. 'Going', Nisha had seen at once, meant 'being got rid of', that in Deepali's absence Hiro will marry off Sudhakar to someone else. Deepali is shaken but is sure Sudhakar will not abandon her. Didn't he have his laboriously constructed image of virility to keep up?

But Sudhakar is not, has never been, a straight 'yes' or 'no' man. Deepali sees it all over again. Subterfuge and trickery for saving face are his natural devices for coping with problems. Whoever succeeds her would be somehow squeezed into the same position as her own. The bonds of wifehood fall off Deepali once and for all. This is where 'with absolute clarity' she sees her decision not to come back 'forming in her with swift, sure strides'.

This intense inner gaze of Deepali is one of those spells of mimesis that recur in Seth's narratives, reinforcing their statements. From the frozen body postures, speech filters in an *abhinaya* of the story by the mime player, and the implications of the excesses suffered by the player.

We join Deepali in her contemplation of her basic state of friendlessness, in a spontaneous arousal of human, not necessarily feminist, feelings intended and achieved by the narrative.

What happens to the Deepalis of our society after their breakaways?

This question shapes the theme of the story ('Usi Jangal Mein'), 'The Same Jungle Again', and the answer worked out by the unnamed woman protagonist forms the climax. She is driven by a compelling, irrational force to go back to the home of the man she had left, give succour to the woman he has deluded and made pregnant, the woman who wishes her to divorce that man to legitimise her unborn child. The protagonist does not know what kind of help she can give. She will not give the woman the divorce she seeks. She doesn't think the right to grant divorce ever was hers: for she never felt married to the man she was married to.

In this jungle of negativities that assail her and shut all lines of action, there is one positive factor she cannot dismiss or disown. It is her body—similar to the other woman's, subjected to the same assaults and battering at the hands of the same man. She is connected to this woman, no matter she is her *saut*, 'the other woman', her enemy. She is connected because their bodies are 'bleeding from the same places, the same wounds'.

The sane, reasoned voice of the narrator abuts here, at this point, threading through the tired, even if persevering, voice of the protagonist. This pervasive voice lifts that statement from the personal to the ethical level. The question of gender is subsumed by the question of the morality of inflicting pain. By what written or unwritten law does one human being get the right to inflict pain upon another?

The protagonist is still nameless, but acquires a face now, the face of one subjected to regular, physical abuse, a face heavy with the scars of the body drained into the mind and the soul.

This kind of ravaged face, and the person possessing it, form the well-spring of the story 'Yatra'. The protagonist is a man. His fetters are not—cannot be—gifts bequeathed by the brainwashing of ideal wifehood. They have come up by his own romantic, adolescent and feudal readings of the employee-employer relationship. It is not contractual, by his reckoning. By these readings, it is a life-long pledge of service and loyalty, of body and mind, by the one to the other.

There are other differences too. The protagonist of 'Yatra' is not as cruelly solitary, as totally estranged from his surroundings as that of 'The Same Jungle Again' or 'Not Without Reason'. He does have the solace of seeing his feelings reciprocated by his masters even if in a measured, formal way, far less ardent than his. And he does have an emotional anchor, an emotional outlet in his son, whatever their differences. Such avenues of exteriorising anguish, it may be said, are instances of male privilege that remain operative even in adverse circumstances. The totally gagged, stifled, and anonymised state of Deepali or the unnamed woman of 'Jungle' is unthinkable for a man unless he is pathological. Neither Deepali, nor the others, it should be noted, are pathological, for all their stifled condition. Their battles are exclusively women's battles that find no aid at hand, no ground support, whatever the informed opinion on the issues concerned. *Therefore,* this reasoning can run, there is no common ground between the first two stories and 'Yatra': that feminist modes are not transcended, it can be argued.

But how does one account for the markedly feminine texture and rhetoric of the 'Yatra' protagonist's vow to kill himself to liberate his son from the life of servitude to the *maaliks* the boy cannot shake off, for all his brightness and promise? The room he and his father live in is the maaliks'. The food they eat is bought from the wage the father gets from the maaliks. And the boy cannot simply quit, leaving his sick father to slog away.

'You won't call this suicide, will you son? The sin of this killing will not taint me ... You will understand ... My heart is overflowing with love for you, brimming and overflowing ... '

The pleading, imploring tone of that address to his son catches the reader's ear at once. The tone etches the face of the speaker in our minds, a face reaching out, eyes fixed and urging, seeking a blending of minds, and his and his son's bodies. This kind of desire for union by the roots has a feminine quality about it, a feminine tenacity. Its compelling physical character is expressed in other places of the story too, where the ailing, ageing father, overcome by emotion, enfolds his son in an embrace. The son's reactions to these bursts of demonstrative love from his usually brooding, lost-looking father are described thus by the writer: 'He folded that touch like a precious cloth and tucked it away within him'. 'Such fondling and caressing ... He closed his eyes and bathed in the waves of the pleasure ... '

The predominantly physical nature of these sensations later develops into a fervour that becomes more than physical, becomes a non-dualist closeness that invokes the biological, interlocked state of the mother and her child in the womb. 'He wanted to hold him against his breast and enfolding him call upon his own death. If he died thus, bearing his love with him in both hands, he'd be reborn within his son in the next life ... '

The feminine function of bearing life is transposed to the male protagonist in a smooth creative glide nullifying the gender factor.

Gender enters these stories in a subtler way than through playing up the woman issue. The writer travels from feminisms to the feminine factor, the feminine component, or the feminine reality in life, conceptualised culturally as *Shakti*. Involuntarily falling in line with the human predisposition to endow physical phenomena with male or female attributes, Seth endows pain with either a feminine or masculine aspect that operates outside the framework of human gender. The pain of 'Yatra's' protagonist is not different from the pains that the women protagonists of 'Reason', 'Jungle', or 'Morass' are prepared to face *after* their immediate problems have been settled one way or another. Deepali's decision to leave Sudhakar seems to make for a complete story, with no prologue waiting in the wings. But in the intense, self-observing gaze that author Seth gives her in another instance of the mimeses that punctuate her writing, we see her waking simultaneously to the dire problems of being the separated woman. Yet she does not backtrack. She will face the problems. They would not, of course, be special to her, to Deepali. They would be the problems of all women like her. But the personal and the collective blend in the inner reaches of Seth's overall narrative temper, dovetailing into the impersonal feminine persona that Seth gives to pain in these stories.

Aartee of 'Morass' transits overnight to the stolid and able woman determined to hold up her home threatening to collapse, when her husband goes away on a risky business venture flouting all her well-founded, rational arguments against it. Why does Aartee take this trouble of propping up an establishment, a system, from which she has received nothing but humiliation?

One can, of course, put it down to her basic, woman's instincts of home-making, of keeping family and home going at all costs. But read the lines again, in the slow, three-dimensional way that all reading requires, and you wake to the impersonality of Aartee's decision to keep the home from falling apart, keep herself from closing the doors of her mind to her husband, despite his ego-driven ways.

Nothing of this turbulence spills over outside. In yet another instance of mimesis we get an inner view of the workings of Aartee's mind. The essential Aartee will, by her own muscle and sinew, 'gather into her hands the four corners of the home threatening to fly apart'. She will do it by herself. She asks 'only herself' for the strength to do this, none else. She will do it for the unwritten, universal principle by which wanton destruction of any kind is abhorrent. Left to themselves, her husband and her sister-in-law would bring about precisely this wanton destruction of the home. This new Aartee, taking birth from the old, will shoulder her task of re-founding her home not only for herself and her interests, but for a principle, for a cause, in a spirit of impersonality.

The militancy and desire for getting even that is associated with feminism is absent in this image of the active, striving woman sketched by the author. The fruits of Aartee's activism are not directed at alleviating chronic women's grievances, but at founding a home-space, a home-area that makes better human beings of its members, both men and women, breeds better relations between them, gives them the strength to hold their own against the stresses of life without loss of scruples.

Aartee's story is not a feminist story but the story of virile femininity. There is a virile, fighting quality to the tableau of her holding up the walls of the home to save it from collapse. But it is a protective gesture at the same time. Concern and anguish underlie its muscular strength. It is more the image of the immanent feminine force that we see in that tableau than feminist aggressiveness.

The feminist fury is more sustained in 'Jungle', is kept in a more unmediated form. The battered-up and runaway protagonist, spare of speech, seething within, and, unnamed, remains thus till almost the end. Very importantly, she is masochistic. She has plucked out from within her all her rightful affections for her own child so as not to deprive it of the ease it is enjoying, ease she cannot afford in her circumstances. Masochism, as feminist theoreticians point out, is a condition highly likely to afflict a woman in the grip of feminist passions. But ironically it is this very streak of self-destruction and the pleasure of pain it rears that bring release to the nameless woman. Erased of name, but indestructible of form, she makes her way to the other woman, manhandled like her, 'bleeding from the same places, the same wounds'. The ego-induced pain of masochistic feminism, by this action of hers, by this 'blood bonding' she makes with the other woman, becomes an ego-free odyssey in search of other, perhaps shared, realities.

The feminine temper, as seen in the uphill tasks undertaken by these women, is more important to Seth than abrasive, one-dimensional feminist attitudes, however necessary they may be at one stage of the story concerned. Also, this feminine aspect, she says, need not be subject to the gender divide. The male protagonist of 'Yatra', in his supplications to his son, evokes the feminine aspect; the hard options that the female protagonists of the stories considered here go in for, and their outward fling of mind, evoke the masculine.

Feminist fervours mellow in Seth's fictional ethic. They expand into humanist statements that transcend gender.

one

Meeting

The bell rang. 'Go in', the *chaprasi* told him: his turn it was now. For hours he'd sat on the hard wooden bench, head bent. Probably dozed off too … In the morning he'd been to the wholesale shop and collected his stock of faggot discards. He had carried the shabby bundle, wrapped in newspaper, in his arms when he came in. He'd shoved it under the bench and planted his foot upon it, to keep it from wobbling. He didn't want the thing seen by others. When the chaprasi told him that he'd been called in, it didn't quite sink in. The prolonged wait had taken the edge off his urgency. In the lounge, the melee of audience-seekers had slowly got sorted out. He rose. The chaprasi opened the spring door. He stepped in. The scene within didn't register at first. Cool, comfortable, well-padded—the exact opposite of the setting he'd been in all this while.

Facing him was the Collector, seated in his chair. The name was Ramdayal Tripathi, he'd heard. He'd heard too about the kind and generous nature of this high official. *And* he'd heard that he would go to any length to resettle any uprooted man, woman or child, in any area of his administrative domain.

Yet …

Yet he felt, stepping inside, that this exemplary Collector too, would not be entirely free of scorn for him. There was no escaping getting face to face with scorn at every turn. Scorn was to be his lot in life.

He gazed at Tripathijee. He saw no scorn there. He saw tenderness. He saw a face soft yet mature with experience.

'Please sit down', he heard this face say.

He hung back at first, but sat, finally. His own towering figure seemed rude to him, seemed set off more by the much shorter seated officer.

'What brings you here, *Shrimanjee*'?

He sat on with lowered eyes. The Collector woke to his blunder. He changed tack, re-framed the question. 'Where did you live over there, which city?'

'Lahore.'

'Are you still in camp or … ?' Tripathijee left his question hanging in the air.

'No. I've taken a two-room house on rent. In Haajeejee's building.'

'Is it good, livable?'

A wavering 'Yes … '

Now? After this? An awkward silence. Probably the Collector Saheb thought that since he was the one who'd come, he should be the one to speak, open his mouth. He was the needy one. Only the man who's thirsty comes to the well.

The silence didn't break, so the Saheb asked: 'What is it you want done?'

'Some means of livelihood, a small job to help me go on. So many things are under rationing these days … maybe a ration shop … '

'How many are there in your family?'

'Some six or seven people. We live together'.

'Any boys?'

'Two. One is a child yet. Born late in my life.'

A man in uniform, like a peon, came in now. In his hands was a big cardboard box. He put it near the visitor, as though he didn't have to be told who its recipient was to be.

'It's for you. Please take it.'

'What is in it?'

'Just a few things, to help you along—as relief.'

'I don't want relief. I want work.'

His voice shook badly.

'There's nothing special in it. Some *atta*, some rice, tea, soap, sugar and so on. Just little things of everyday need. Take it along for now. Open the box and show him, Balbir.'

The man stretched out his hand and stopped the employee from opening the box, from displaying its contents for his benefit. He sat pressed flat against the back of the chair. And he sat straight, departing from his usual posture of sitting slumped, eyes down. He locked his hands behind his head. The erect posture now threw into full relief his imposing build. His face-to-face session with the high official suddenly seemed momentous.

But no attempt at speaking seemed forthcoming from him as yet. The bureaucrat now turned bureaucrat, straight and simple, with no frills.

'Say something, my good sir. What are you thinking about so deeply?'

'I'm thinking … thinking, and thinking, that in those deadly riots, everyone's children died. Why didn't mine too? Why did they stay alive? All of them … '

He faltered: his words tapered away. He bit back without success a sob clamouring for escape. His cheeks moistened with unstoppable tears. He wasn't awake enough even to hide his shame of weeping in public. Not awake enough even to know that he was playing false with his own words, that he was turning tail, backtracking.

How did he forget that'd he'd spoken these very thoughts he'd blubbered now, had spoken them with ardour, zeal, in this very life, under this very sky? Driven by this very heart and mind of his. Spoken them with a different vision, different conviction.

Not many days had passed to make him forget—make him forget what he'd said to his weeping wife. Said at the time they were leaving their family home. In Lahore. Now in Pakistan. Again and again his wife had turned back to look at their receding home, tears flooding her face. Her sobs were soft and suppressed, for her father-in-law was with them. But her soft sobs hammered in his breast. Her companion for life, he heard and read his wife's language.

He stopped, at a loss for any other course of action. He shut his eyes to the presence of his father walking a few steps ahead. He clutched his wife's wrist. Tightened his grip. With his other hand he raised her chin. He said sternly: 'You are not leaving behind any home or homestead, you know it. You are going to *your* country, carrying your greetings of freedom to Pandit Nehru. You are fortunate. Thank your stars. People have lost whole families. You've lost none … '

All this he had said. While leaving home, clutching his wife's hand. With full conviction, full faith. Just about six months ago, in this year now going past. In this life. Under this sky. Bearing this very head, this very heart. In this short stretch of time does a man change? Does history beat and pound a man into another man—into a man so malleable, helpless?

None of these things could Tripathijee know. Despite sympathy and generosity, the festering, throbbing pain bred in camps and caravans was beyond the grasp of a desk-bound officer.

Tripathijee was kind, therefore he saw. He listened too. And provided hospitality. And he also controlled with ease and grace the crowds milling at his door day after day, drawn by his innovative act of putting together hampers of everyday articles for the afflicted. For so many days, for so many months, he'd performed this selfless deed unstintingly.

Seeing this strange visitor of his broken as visibly as a gaping wound sent him into god knew what thoughts. He saw the tall, burly, proud man sitting there across the table, gone blubbery as a child with sobs and tears. He hadn't said anything to cause this … hadn't spoken any harsh words … then why, why … ?

The man didn't give time to Tripathijee for thinking more. He rose to his feet. 'Pardon me, sir', he raised his hand in salutation, and came out of the room. He forgot his bundle of faggots under the bench which he was to take home to light the hearth. How was the fire going to be lit now? The sawdust kept as a standby had got spent long ago.

two

My Option

It is decided. The places to see today are Rajghat and Lal Quila. Why not go to Palika Bazar again today, I had suggested.

Yesterday had been a fiasco. The lights failed. The humid evening, the airless corridors, the reek of human bodies, doubts about the quality of the drinking water available, and above all the power failure in that air-conditioned fortress just put the lid on everything. Not that Ashwini had been grumpy or short tempered. With the two children, he had loitered happily enough around the makeshift tea stalls to the right of Palika Bazar: moving off, now to the fly-ridden push carts selling cane juice, now towards the dug-up roads, now gazing with interest at the four-seater drivers spouting abuses nonstop.

In the shade of the stairway roof, Nilima stood watching silently.

'Call the children over, why don't you? Mucking around in the dirt!' I said.

'Let them. Let them wallow in it.'

'Are those tea stalls any place for wallowing in?' I persisted.

'Don't ask me. Ask Ashwini. He's the one wallowing and mucking around.'

Dirty water sluiced out of the tea stall opposite. Brown and brothy after washing cups and saucers, it sent the two children skittering. But not before Sonia's expensive frock was spattered with mud from Sunny's wet shoes. Sonia set up a scream. Her screams left Nilima unmoved, the baby in her arms.

'Go on. Tag along some more behind your father,' she flared up.

'Neeloo! Is anything the matter between you and Ashwini?' I gathered the courage to ask. Since yesterday I had been postponing the question, even though nothing could be postponed, really. There was no time for postponements. Three weeks they had, a precious three weeks in which they had planned trips to Kathmandu, Bhopal and Agra over and above their Delhi round. There were relatives to be visited. Friends. And shopping of course. Neeloo was here after thirteen years. Gone away that long ago, and coming again now, with three children. She'd gone away plump and come back thin. Ashwini had gone away thin and come back plump.

'Nothing's the matter between Ashwini and me.' She changed my question into an answer and handed it back to me. With a dry, detached voice.

I was embarrassed. Ashwini came back with the children.

'Why is there no light in there, Uncle?' Sunny looked at me, eyes limpid.

'That's the way it is over here,' answered Ashwini.

'*Not* uncle, say *Mamajee*,' Nilima almost shrieked. 'Making an uncle of anyone and everyone.' Blind hatred stirred in her voice, reined in tight.

I thought she was getting worked up for nothing.

By consensus, the day is not to be frittered away at Palika Bazar to make up for yesterday's fiascos. Rajghat and the Red Fort are to be done today—via the Ring Road.

'Stop! Stop!' Ashwini, happily humming in the car whizzing down Ring Road, suddenly calls out. I brake the car with a screech.

'What is it now?' Neeloo interjects like a policewoman. 'Why have you stopped the car? What do you have to do? Let's get to Rajghat fast … '

'Come Sunny!' Ashwini is rapt, not seeming to have heard. He's opened the car door and taken Sonia in tow too. Round his neck dangles his camera, ever there. 'Hurry.'

The three troop off, forgetting us. Us meaning Mother, Neeloo, the baby and me. Neeloo's face suddenly turns hard and still, rock-like.

'Relax. Why are you so tense?'

I am always forced to say such things in English. These ready-made expressions cannot be uttered in Hindi, making Mother feel all at sea.

On Neeloo's face is a raging but mute agitation. She looks sometimes in front, sometimes behind. Then she gets out of the car and stands leaning against the bonnet.

Out there across the road Ashwini is dashing along, holding the children by their hands. He clambers up and down raised spots on the ground one after the other. Finally, he stands steady on one and adjusts his camera. And then he seems to want to leave the spot. Where he stands, runs a wall straight in front of him, made of battered tin sheets stretching far down, cheek by jowl with the electric pole. From where we are, the scene on the other side of the wall is hidden. What could be there? What is it that is holding Ashwini in thrall thus? I too want to see the source of his excitement, and get ready to seek a proper place to look out from, when Neeloo pulls me back by the arm.

'Have you too lost your head like Ashwini?'

'Why? What have I done?'

'Nothing.' She goes quiet, seeing me stop, and opens the car door to be with Mother.

Far away, standing at a carefully selected level, Ashwini is seen photographing the scene behind the wall of tin sheets. Sunny seems set on making him lose his footing, for he keeps pulling at him by the belt of his jeans. Ashwini wards him off again and again. Sunny thrashes about wildly. Suddenly he pushes extra hard at Ashwini just about to click his camera, which makes him lose focus.

Perhaps the shot has been spoilt, for Ashwini loses his cool. In a rage he smacks Sunny hard, setting him howling. He prepares to run towards the car but Ashwini pulls him back by the hand and smacks him again.From behind his face another face has reared up: 'That'll teach you to misbehave!'

Neeloo comes running out of the car and stops Aswhini's hand midway, about to strike again. 'Stop hitting him! And stop taking it out on him! You think I can't see?'

'So what *you* can see? It's these blighted idiots who have to see! How will they ever know what they would have got in life, and what they are getting now! Will they will never count their blessings?'

Neeloo cuddles Sunny, blind to Ashwini, shaken by a burst of god knows how many suppressed rages. And Ashwini, at ease after his outburst, goes back to his camera, all concentration.

I see everything in scattered, disconnected scenes. There's no running link. Something stirs within me. I can't put my finger on it.

'Neeloo, come out.' Who is this person within me ordering around my sister two years my senior? I don't know. Neeloo doesn't seem roused to any kind of movement. She leans out a little from the window, and keeps sitting where she is. Rooted.

'Don't you hear me?' I think saying this should be enough to shake her out of herself. But she does not move, seated beside her mother. This stubbornness stirs a quick flash of anxiety within me. It has to go, of course—and it does—for Ashwini is back with a bounce and has sat in the car. Pleased with himself. Humming.

Everybody is content, drinking in the lovely grassy expanse of the Gandhi Memorial at Rajghat. Green, downy lawns, spotless, well-paved pathways, the tingle of cool grass on feet set free of shoes. The crunch of gravel underfoot. Flowers and fragrance. '*Hé Ram*'—the two words etched on gleaming black stone, above the cross-legged posture of Gandhi.

'Ashwini, come here. Take a photograph of this.' Neeloo goes warm suddenly. Her face softens, clear of tension.

But Ashwini is not there. Neeloo has taken an about-turn to look at him. He is not in sight anywhere. Where has he wandered off again? Again and again ... ?

Mother seems to have come upon a special holy task to perform, a task kept in readiness for her. Bowing repeatedly, hands folded, circumambulating, she is in a trance. I am unable to do anything. I can only gaze at Neeloo, Neeloo bereft of hope, Neeloo drained out, Neeloo sobbing away within.

'Come, let's walk.' I hold her hand. She lets her hand be in mine—perhaps for some comfort—but when had there ever been any such solid bridges between us? How could they have been built? These past thirteen years we have lived in our own spheres, in our own ways, reposing a simple trust in the natural bond of our relationship. She had been married off thirteen years ago, the same year in which father's illness had been diagnosed as cancer. I remember to this day her sobbing without end. She saw a harsh connection between her father's grappling with death and her being married off. She wanted to live on at home. Father was stubborn. He was getting a rare gem in the form of Ashwini.

The two of us came over from one pavement of the memorial to a second on the other side. We kept within view Mother urging the children again and again to bow their heads.

'How do you feel here, tell me.' I wanted to distract her attention.

'Very good! But why think about feeling good when it's there that you've got to live. Ashwini is better off than me. Forever in search of newer and newer reasons for liking that country. He searches for them everywhere. Here especially. In his own country. Doesn't spare it. No conflict disturbs him. I can't bear it. You tell me, should anyone set fire to one's own little home, because others live in mansions? And what mansions are they anyway? Everyone there seems like a worker to me, a labourer. No real concept of fine living they have there, nothing with roots … '

'Why do you get so personal about it?'

'Isn't the problem of my children personal?'

Ashwini came into view from behind the incline, loping down. The camera danced round his neck and in his hands was a reel of film.

'Where were you?'

'Just here and there. Went to the dump on the other side. I wanted to take photos. I want to show these little rogues with us what good luck it is that we don't live here. In this country of slums.'

'Ashwini!' Neeloo screamed. 'You want your cover-up for living there, fine! But do you know at what cost … '

'See that? See how touchy and irrational your sister is?' Carelessly, he began beating a tattoo on my shoulder.

The fog was lifting from my head. Meaning and coherence came up now, linking scattered scenes. Something like this had happened at the airport too. The moment he was through the gate he'd clasped his own neck with his hands. 'It's choking!'

God knows what he'd seen in the half-lit dark. Perhaps the roads dug up for making the international airport. And just then he found a bag missing from his pile of luggage.

He blew his top straight off. 'I knew exactly these things would happen here! Now it'll never, never be found!'

I tried to calm him, told him that no porter or visitor was allowed inside, so there was little chance of its being stolen. He would get it back. But he brushed aside my attempts at pacification like brushing off a speck of dust from his jacket. Neeloo was standing at a distance, detached from it all. In a grey skirt and maroon scarf. I was seeing her after years. She asked, 'How is Mother?'

'All right now.'

'Thought of coming at that time but … ' She fell silent, not mentioning Father.

'I understand.' The dialogue could have gone on if she hadn't been locked up in some turmoil within.

Ashwini came back with the missing bag, and burst out: 'What makes you so blissfully blind to your surroundings?'

Neeloo didn't reply. She got into the car.

I couldn't tell if his bristling was because of the bag or because of his inability to stay untouched by the grime and dust around.

Coming away from Raj Ghat, on the Ring Road again, Ashwini shouted for the car to stop. He leapt out. His hurried exit set the thermos at his feet rolling. At a level below the sweep of the wide road were rows of *jhuggis* for labourers. Nearby was an expanse for making manure from the city's garbage. And next to it ran a stomach-churning, open drain. Ashwini came back with his photo.

'What rare find have you made, *bhai saheb*?' I asked.

'Everyone gets what he looks for.' Not Ashwini but Neeloo answered my question.

Something hardened within me. Neeloo's eye was becoming my

eye: Neeloo's psyche becoming my psyche—increasingly. She must be enduring these mean, sneaky acts of his, alone and by herself. In alien country, breathing alien air. Far away from her own folk.

I said to myself that I would speak to Neeloo. But what would I tell her? She might well turn a blind eye to the realities of a foreign land. But what about attitudes, the attitudes of the person she was living with? The person who was the only one she could turn to on alien soil? For the first time I saw that a sense of belonging did not come from just a person, but from the air and the soil of one's homeland. Without these a man hugs close to his heart matters not worth a thought.

Ashwini's hand brushing my shoulder startled me.

'What's up, pal? Become your sister's brother with a vengeance?'

'No. It's just a bit of a headache I have.'

He opened the zip of his leather pouch and handed me a packet. 'Here, this is Tylanol, an antidote to the addictive use of aspirin. I bet you folks here don't even know that aspirin is to be avoided.'

What does 'here' mean, I wanted to ask. But I'd never been on that kind of wavelength with Ashwini.

'I'll be all right.' I took his hand off my shoulder.

'Come on, *yaar*,' he pressed the flap of the packet and let the tablet slide into his hand.

'There's no water. The thermos broke.' I put the tablet into my pocket. The matter ended there.

Now Ashwini began humming a tune. Some crisp and fast Western tune. Slapping both thighs and keeping a beat. His tone blended with the tune, fully became one with it. His uttering the words hadn't yet struck this blend.

'You too, Sonia,' he urged the girl sitting at the back to join in. Immediately her piping voice rose, trying to chime with the voices of her father and brother.

Now he was beginning to tap his foot too, and he was swaying.

A picnic-like atmosphere set in. I don't know why, I began to wish for Neeloo's voice to sound in this pleasing family togetherness.

'*Didi*, don't you know this song?' It was Didi I wanted to call her, not Neeloo.

'She does but she won't sing,' Ashwini said, and got back to the singing.

Suddenly his palm clenched my wrist. 'Stop, please, stop the car. And back it a little. Back to the spot we've just come from.'

'You can't stop here.' I was already a little put off.

'O come on, yaar, who cares here, who'll see?'

'What do you mean who cares? We can be *chalaaned*.' I kept the car running, even if slowly. And then I speeded up.

'O, all right, some other time then,' Ashwini shrugged, relaxed.

'I'm told there's a regular sound and light show at the Red Fort,' Neeloo said. 'About the history of the Mughals and the struggle for Independence.'

'Yes, Didi. We are headed there.'

'Didi? You called me "Didi"? Well, well, something I've gained all right, by going out there,' she laughed for the first time.

As soon as the car went past the Daryaganj crossing, Ashwini's eyes got their savage gleam again.

On the bricked footpath bisecting the road in front was a row of shelters minus walls on the sides. The shelters were slung over two poles. Keeping the roofs in place were sheets of tin, canvas and thatch, torn and faded rags, strips of plastic. There were naked children, women with knees and breasts practically bare. Young girls picked lice from each other's hair. Tin boxes and aluminium cooking pots lay round.

A wave of sickness rose within me. Everything showed itself at one glance. Gave more than what it showed. Provided material to Ashwini to feast his eyes on, and to me to sink more into my own self. I seemed to have trouble breathing. A black, wet world closed around me and had me by the neck—held me clamped between countless layers of guilt and shame within my own self. The pain of stumbling upon this world so suddenly, without warning, was so sharp that I almost blacked out. How I would grapple with this awakening was for the future to tell. At this time the only question was of shutting Ashwini's eagle eye.

If only, if only, I had a vast sheet to hang as a curtain between Ashwini's irreverent eyes and this sordid world which was mine too, lying thus sprawled naked before me. But I felt disabled, incapable of action.

'Stop the car, yaar, stop it dead,' Ashwini crowed, insistent. 'You're just not listening.'

'I am listening.' I speeded up the car more.

I was incapable of doing anything else, but I could use the steering wheel in my hands the way I wished. This wheel was no more now to go to the places Ashwini wanted. It was to go to the places I wanted.

three

Amma's Gold

She is awake: jerks awake every night. In the first quarter of the night she nods off. After that it's the *thak-thak* of the *chowkidar*'s lathi, the keening of the dogs closing in and fading out, the all-enveloping, dense, dark. When the temple bells set up their peals, she senses daybreak.

But tonight even the first quarter's sleep has failed her. Last evening's news has shaken her. Death has struck again in Kargil. Fourteen *jawans* killed. Tomorrow or the day after, their bodies will be brought home. The news, read out in standard, stock phrases, has set her trembling. Old pains are reincarnating in the new ones. You can't badger the new pain, 'I know you, dog -face! I know you too well. Get lost!' Every new pain demands a new name for itself, a new garb.

Kargil has re-awakened sleeping pains, sleeping since God knows when. Her mind, in defiance of her wish, refuses to disconnect from the news coming in from over there, from the Kargil sector. With the death of each jawan, a coil of her guts straightens out. She is surprised—so much uncoiling had not taken place even at that time when the sky caved in on her, when her firstborn, Vijay, went down in the China war. Does grief go thin because of the tag of martyrdom? Things were different in that war. On the snow-capped hills the jawans died, and that was all. When and where they died, when and where the bodies were found and picked up, no one knew. For some days reports saying 'whereabouts unknown' would keep coming. And then, a special news item: a special shock.

From Vijay's unit too, one evening two men came with special news. They stood looking at her with a special look. Then one of them stepped forward and clasped her to himself. 'You are the mother of a martyr, *Ammajee.* Vijay has stolen a march over us, his pals.'

The information was complete, her readiness to meet it was not. She stood. Still. Not crying, not breaking into lament. One of the men held her suddenly-icy hands in his: 'Ammajee, Vijay is gone but we are your sons too'.

They left. She never saw them again. Nehru was making incessant appeals to the women for ornaments, appealing to them to part with their gold for the country. She did not respond or react. She had donated her most precious ornament.

On the TV screen, she sees the patchwork of news. The smoke of gunfire rises from the craggy hills of Kargil. Even sitting in the room, she feels that the thick black smoke is choking her. The jawans run and she runs with them. They load their cannon and she loads the weapons with them. Everything is happening right where she is sitting, right in front of her on the screen. Tough-looking jawans. Fragments of bodies tied into bundles. Boxes draped with the tricolour. Flowers. Salutes. Ministers. State honours. Names of villages of birth. Statements of mothers and fathers: brave statements by the fathers, holding down the mute trembling of their hearts, 'laid down his life for his motherland, my son did ... blessed am I.'

She is giddy. Digs into her own flesh, in every part of her body to find where lies the sharp end of the pain of that time. If Vijay's body had been found and brought home with such pomp, would the pain have been a little less?

Nothing is clear. Pain spreads, keeps spreading. Tears begin to flow, keep on flowing. The wounds of those days weep now. How does water seep from rocks? Has old age gone berserk? Has it made time and space rain down on her in a combined deluge? She has all the time in the world now for crying.

She hadn't had it then. Her husband had died nine months before. Vijay just martyred, Beenoo a child yet. You need time and space for crying. She had had neither. The boulders of responsibility had crushed her.

Left to herself, she'd want to see nothing but these events she is seeing on the TV screen. But it is not left to her. Everyone has her own taste, her own demand over and above the news. She hears what she can, what is allowed, and comes back to her room to stretch her limbs. The hunger for news gnaws at her without let or hindrance.

Under the mattress she has stashed away some old newspaper sheets. Her bed is her only sanctuary. The clusters of pictures on the pages grip her attention. She will look at the pictures freely and long when everyone has gone, she thinks. But no, there is no seeing them freely and long even then. The papers have slid under the mattress. Her cot has become a hammock from her nightly, insomniac huddles upon it. The papers shift and rustle under her body. Clasping her knees, putting her weight on one elbow, she tries to pull the papers out. But midway, her waist freezes in an arch. She thrashes about for all she is worth, but where's the heat for unfreezing the arch? Breathlessness takes over and butts the walls of her heart like bellows. She turns ashen. The bout of pain lasts two whole days. The twisted muscle at the waist throbs away, a pain of its own.

The papers are a sodden mass. Even if she'd managed to gather them into her hands, her glasses wouldn't have done their job. She brings the papers very near her eyes, till they brush the frame of her glasses. But she sees nothing. Black spots swarm and prance before her eyes. In a fright she puts the papers down, just touches them, feels them. Her hands stroke their surface. Her eyes see her hands stroking, but convey no meaning. When Eeshaan comes back from school, he will read them out to her, though she knows that her glasses are bent from Eeshaan's scuffling with her some days before, raging at his grandmother for being nabbed to read out the paper.

For quite some time she's been watching Eeshaan straining to break free. He doesn't meet her eye now. She keeps watch over his movements, his meal times, his play hour. He just has to edge past her, and she has him by the collar. After that, it is coaxing and cajoling, and even bribing … a few raisins thrust into his hand. 'Read on, son, read a little more. Tell me a little more, son.'

Eeshaan reads out as though reciting a school lesson. It's no reading out he does, just a disgorging of words. Scolding him, trying to halt the flow, she wants to get back to the same news and headline, wants to get back to the same scenes they evoke. Eeshaan is sick of this repetition. He looks for ways of escape. Of late he has acquired a new interest. In his list of news for reading out to *Daadee*, he has included Amitabh Bachchan. Again and again he reads the publicity puffs for the 'Veer Jawan Fund' of the Defence Campaign.

The ad throws her off balance. Morning , evening and noon, the same message is put out on *Doordarshan*. The newspapers are following suit. She hears that on the post office walls too the same advertisement is being pasted. On lamp posts at crossroads, at bus stops, at the railway station, on the notice boards of children's schools, the same ad, the same message.

Her heart breaks. It means, then, that the government is in a spot! The government is asking for help! The government is in dire straits. The government does not know how long the war will go on, how many men will die, how many will be injured, how much food and how much arms will have to be sent out to the lads there. How many corpses will have to be brought home …

On the joints of her aging bones, the stomp of military boots begins its dance. Basking in the sun, knees half bared, she sits leaning against the wall. Eeshaan goes on reading. Like a pendulum she swings with the words. Eeshaan is reading out, she repeats them to herself.

' … he too likes Hindi film songs like you. He too likes the scent of rain on parched earth. He too cries like you when Amitabh Bachchan "dies" … '

Eeshaan stops all of a sudden. 'I don't suppose you've even heard of Amitabh Bachchan, Daadee?'

Eeshaan sees that Daadee is not listening. Head against the wall, eyes closed, she is sitting like a statue. On the folds of her face moisture glistens. He stops reading. He knows that when he stops Daadee at once wakes up with a rush of words. But today Daadee is not speaking. Elated at this godsent opportunity, he runs out to play and to freedom.

She knows that there is more left to the message. It is about to come to its real point. It wants to say, 'He too has dreams for his children like you. But among the Unknowns for whom he has gone to die, is You'.

How will Eeshaan know where in its flight upward a rhythm breaks? How will he know which branch of the tree of memory quivers in which corner of the mind?

At night, when she comes in to sleep, her mind is crushed as if from weeping. The past has dug a tunnel, she feels. It has prised out with iron tongs her life secreted away in an old dank bundle somewhere. Tonight would be another sleepless night, she feels sure. But it doesn't turn out so. Sleep comes the minute she lies down, perhaps from sheer exhaustion.

Birds call. Temple bells ring. She wakes. The waking also wakes the words read out by Eeshaan, as if she had slept with them. And alongside wakes also a belief, tightening its grip. 'This is something even I can do. I can also give to the Defence Fund. I will rest easy afterwards.' It wouldn't be the earth she would be giving. The earth is not hers to give, nor are its living and dying. But some amount of money is definitely within her power to give.

What amount?

She stops in her tracks. Drained of hope. What amount? She is alive to her less than limited capacity, to her pitiable have-not state. Beenoo has set up home here, in Kanpur, and she has become part of it. The Bareilly house that had borne the stamp of her mistress-ship has slipped out of her hands. This house here in Kanpur is Beenoo's and Rashmi's. Here her rank and standing, like any old woman's, is below those of Eeshaan and Eshaa. She has never had to put it to the test so far. She thinks of Ramkalee, who had asked for seven hundred rupees for her daughter's marriage. Since it wasn't for herself, she had asked Beenoo freely without hesitation. She hadn't expected him to refuse, not the way he did, at least. He called Ramkalee a beggar and a scrounger—an exploiter of the large-heartedness of her employer's dotard of a mother. He would throw the woman out, he raged, if she went on in this way.

She had tried to argue. But how could Beenoo know the kind of understanding there was between her and Ramkalee? On the earnings of this beggar, Ramkalee, the semblance of a home was running. She had looked to Rashmi for support. But Rashmi stood silent, in full agreement with her husband.

Anger seized her. And she spoke up. 'That's enough, Beenoo, pipe down, just pipe down. Don't go on and on. Your father's pension is still coming in. Just keep that in mind!'

'So what? You think your medicines come free?'

She was struck dumb. How low could a man go? How mean could mean be? She was the one to retreat, bide her time for the wounds to heal.

But this thing that they are faced with today, this thing is not just about a Ramkalee. It is about the whole country. The way her heart is aching, aching away without a pause, wouldn't Beenoo's heart too be aching the same way? Even otherwise, giving has its own dignity, its own grace. There must be something in the air that's bringing in the money from all sides. This oneness being shown today, isn't it a purging of the soul of the country?

Her heart feels light like cotton fleece. Fleece is light. But just gin it, and this light substance fluffs out so much, so-o-o much that you don't know where to store it. Her heart feels light like that, like cotton ginned.

The morning tasks glide along fast now. Her knees are where they always are, doing well what they always do—aching, acting up. Only, she is not with them. She waters the *tulsi* plant, feeds the birds, and then sits down to her beads. But her heart is so charged today the beads don't so much as move, stay stuck in her fingers like pellets of wood. Flustered, she puts them away.

Within her a thought chases, harries. Her eyes loop Beenoo, turn when he turns, still when he does. When would that electric instant come when she can lay before his smug male power this wish swelling from the loamy soil of her mind?

She is looking for a chance. She gets it. She saunters up to where he sits shaving. Beenoo shaves in the open, seated on a rope cot—never in the bathroom like his father—staring into the mirror fixed on the lid of an old wooden box.

She feels no need for a formal opening. And she doesn't make any preamble.

'I want money, Beenoo. Some five thousand rupees.'

'Money? Five thousand!'

How can Beenoo not give a start? Such cheek from so crumpled a package, like Maa! After all these years!

'For what?'

'For something … anything … '

'You don't tell, you don't get.'

'If I tell, I get?'

'Possibly.' Beenoo goes on with his shaving.

'I want to give to the Defence Fund.'

'We've already given to the Defence Fund! Money's gone on behalf of me, Rashmee, the children!'

'Why not on my behalf?'

Beenoo falters a second and then reasons sweetly, 'Are you and we different, mother?'

'We are, yes, on this. You can understand it if you want to.'

A knot forms in her throat. If she speaks on, her cloak of dignity will be in shreds. She will look like a beggar.

'This is futile talk, mother. Rashmee and I have each contributed one day's salary. The two children have given in money at the school. We gave Eeshaan a hundred rupees, but he thought it below his dignity. He has to show off. He wants to match the rich brats! They all do, vie with each other to be the champion show-off. Do you know how much Eeshaan took? Full two hundred and fifty rupees! And Eeshaa! You think she is any less? She wants as much, not a paisa less! Crisp new notes she has taken! As if those very notes would be sent to the jawaans!'

And I? I have no duty or desire of my own? The words hovered on her lips but were not spoken.

Her silence makes Beenoo raise his eyes and look at her. The face is ashen, pallid like the earth without sap. Eyes the colour of soot. The skin below the left cheek hangs loose—from one side only, at that. From lack of dental care, perhaps. He feels he is looking at her face after years, no matter they've been living in the same house.

'You've given your son, Amma! China or Kargil, what's the difference?'

Her heart grows heavy. It has been a wasteland for years. But something like a sob strains against her mouth. She turns her face away, sits down on the frame of the cot.

'We'll see in the evening.' Beenoo gets up, looking at his watch.

There is something about Beenoo's behaviour that keeps her in a reverie the whole day. Beenoo has remembered his brother! After years! Remembered him today. He has recalled his brother as brother, over and above the son lost to his mother. In earlier days she would have rushed to make for him the sweet *puris* he liked! What other means has she ever had to make herself known to Beenoo?

But the evening that Beenoo means never comes, never comes on any evening. Even on the second and third days the silence continues. She feels cheated. Cheated by Beenoo. He has simply handed her a balloon of the past that stays afloat with the gas filling its plastic belly. She is as empty-handed as ever, as penniless. A film of pulpy scum envelops her mind. The scum becomes like amoeba. It spreads and joins up with other happenings of the past. This joining up doesn't feel good. Between her two eyes, which are like her two sons, the space widens, keeps widening. She feels that from within Beenoo a thoughtless egoism is emerging. The remoter the death becomes, the more of an 'other' his brother grows. He has his brother's share of the family property. He has his own ample earnings. And he has the legacy of his forefathers. This river of wealth flowing serenely behind him has suddenly taken a leap forward and plunged into a well, in the waters of which he sees only his own reflection, only his. He is growing vain—vain like an only son. How expensive this vanity is, acquired at what cost—doesn't he know? On the masthead of this vanity of his flutters the rag of pain.

He has been evading her since that day when he'd said, 'We'll see in the evening.' She perceives this only too well. Yesterday he was supposed to have had a headache. When she went in he was flopped on the bed, a hand flung over both eyes. Not a syllable of welcome, not a sound escaped him. Staying anywhere near him was out of the question. She turned back. When she lay down at night after her meal, she thought they were playing cards. Peals of laughter streamed out of their room. For a young husband and wife, caught every minute of their lives in the unlovely business of making money, was this the only pleasure available in the heady secrecy of night?

Beenoo's attitude and behaviour torment her. Humiliate her. Why did she ask? Why did she put her hand out? Why did she appeal to a rich skinflint like Beenoo? She has debased her request, sullied her petition.

Is she groping for a true picture of her standing in the house? Or is she confirming her worst fears by diagnosing and dissecting Beenoo? She doesn't know. Her mind is befogged. The humiliation of begging, her helpless state, the changes made by time … to which prong of this multi-pronged fork could she say, '*You*, YOU hurt me more!'

What she had prayed for was the power to emerge from the deep pit of swamp and marsh she was trapped in, with the fever of her desire. She had prayed that in this great *yagna* of the war, even her small offering would be sanctified by her firm will and resolve, would not be subjected to humble supplications from her. She had prayed for strength to her passion.

All the four quarters of the night she has been awake. Sleep plays truant. First there was the pain of her helplessness, then the flickering gleam of seeing a way out, and then, the frenzy of waiting for daybreak. Each phase of the mental process scraped the skin of sleep like a razor, but she is not spent, far from it. Ever since getting up she has been looking for a chance to confront Beenoo.

She gets it as he sits in the verandah, newspaper in hand. On the table in front she sees two empty cups. Rashmee must have had her tea already, and gone in to get ready for office.

Holding on to the back of the vacant cane chair, she moves up and sits. All this action makes a noise. He can hear it if he wants to. But he has to want to.

Today she will not wait for his wanting or not wanting. Today there is a stir in her mind, a ticking away after years, a tiny spark dancing in the stale heap of her body. Today the road ahead does not seem blocked.

Beenoo's pose of intense concentration in the paper makes her laugh a bit, as if in the adult body of Beenoo the imp of childhood still lurks, playing hide and seek. She breaks the silence on her own.

'How dry the grass has become in this fierce heat, hasn't it, Beenoo?'

To address him by name seems necessary. He shouldn't think it is just a passing observation she could be making to anyone.

'Hmmm!' Beenoo grunts. For an instant, he casts a glance at the lawn and then resumes his deep scrutiny of the newspaper.

Does he think she can't understand? But today it is not *she* who has to understand. She has to make *him* understand. By giving over to him the bundle she holds in her hands. In this bundle is money in the form of solid gold, money that is solely hers. A nose-pin along with the four gold bangles of the six given to her on the thirteenth-day rites after Beenoo's father's death. Given to formalise her widowhood. To wear six bangles together seemed ostentatious then, a mockery of her darkened mind. Four she had put away in a box, and two she had slipped on. The nose jewel is a priceless antique, studded with genuine pearl and emerald. It is a memento of her mother's. The radiance of the pearl lights up the wearer's cheek. She recalls this, and feels embarrassed even now. She can't explain how it has remained with her. The cloth in which it had stayed wrapped is as old as her widowhood. As full of the past.

'Here ...,' she says with an attempt at persuasion.

'Why are you giving me this?' Beenoo doesn't even raise his face from his paper, leave alone take the bundle.

But nothing is going to daunt her. She is determined. Salvaging shreds of her womanhood from her tattered motherhood, she says, 'There are four bangles here, and one nose ring.'

Beenoo seems to go into a state of shock, sitting in his chair. He takes the bundle and digs his fingers into the knot.

'Why are you giving this? Do you know the price of gold?'

'I do, that's why. Even if they weigh four *tola*s, twenty thousand rupees you can get easily. We can give to ten defence funds with that money. The nose pin will have to be valued.'

'Have you lost your wits, mother? The children's schooling is still to finish … and this nose ring … where will you ever get the likes of it today?' In the flood of sunshine from the freshly risen day he lifts the jewel and stares with narrowed eyes at the light streaming from it. Perhaps he is estimating its worth.

Ah, but how stupid of her! Stupidity entirely her own! She has never thought that his conceit of seeing himself as master of all would crow out thus from these symbols of her widowhood too. Never has her mind worked along these lines. Never has it struck her that from these bangles of widowhood too, the conceit of sole proprietorship could gloat thus.

Beenoo does not put down the bundle. He twirls the bangles between his fingers, feels their roundness.

'Forget it then, Beenoo. If you are not inclined that way, forget it. Let me have them back.'

'Let them be around here, *maa*. We will put them in the locker tomorrow. Where do you keep them in that dump of a room? The cleaning woman can steal them any time.'

If she, a human being, alive and breathing, can stay in that dump of a room, why not dead gold? But she can't throw such a retort at her son, however driven to it.

She makes her hand her voice, her tongue. She keeps her palm open and extended towards him. A palm stretched thus on an invisible platform of air—motionless, still, a palm demanding the restoration of her rights of ownership.

Beenoo looks at his mother. What he sees he doesn't want to see again. In those eyes the earth is crouching to leap. In this stretching of the hand is an asking that is the claiming of a right that cannot be refused.

He wraps up the bundle and gives it back to her. She rises. And moves away towards her room. She knows that she would definitely find someone who would treat this gold simply as her gold, someone who would not devour it with his eyes, molest it with his hands.

Perhaps the gardener who comes to water the plants can take on the task of selling the gold.

Last year, the good fellow had planted so many herbs right under her window, so many healing herbs to make a warm poultice for her aching knees.

four

Outsiders

Midnight ... An old woman—come up knocking. Knocking, not on the door, but on the broken glass of the bedroom window. And she doesn't exactly knock. She pushes her head in through the big hole in the window.

In the dim light of the balcony outside, her face detached from her body rouses terror, terror not easy to imagine. A neck, no more than a neck, materialises in the whitish dark void around the person lying slack on the bed. From the neck breaks out a voice, suggesting a face. 'Kaka isn't yet home.' The voice, with its suggestion of a face, repeats 'isn't yet' twice, thrice.

Already my moment is gone—the moment that was quivering like a half-formed dream in the waters of sleep. My breathing is coming back to normal.

'What do you mean, "isn't yet?"' I jerk out of bed.

'Don't you know ... ? *Not yet!* See what the time is! Look at your watch.' There is a bite to her voice, a sharp reprimand.

Within me the fog is clearing. And the clarity dispels my terror of a minute ago. I pick up the torch and look at the watch. 'It's twelve already, ten minutes over.'

'Ah-h-h.'

'Your son hasn't yet come back from the office?'

She shakes her head fast and long, like a branch swayed by a storm. Heaven knows how many thousand minutes of anxiety-filled stasis she has flung away in that hysterical movement. When the swaying stops there rises the stifled sound of sobs bit down between the teeth. Then silence.

The curtain on the window moves. A shaft of light flows in from the balcony bulb.

I am alert now, my brain ticking.

Mountains, rain, twisting roads, slopes, tracks without barriers, blind turns, darkness: and cleaving these, the smooth, slithering speed of motorbikes, the heat of blood come of age, or perhaps the smog of booze, or perhaps just habit, habit blunting the keen edge of seeing and grasping—which of these was it?

I have nothing to give the old lady that could bring her at least the illusion of hope. All I have are fears of the direst kind.

Even in this moment of helpless inaction, I feel the eye of hope somewhere from within her regarding me with nervous expectation. Its sharp point drives into me. But I also feel the weevils of helplessness crawling within me. She doesn't know that I too am an outsider here, I don't know anyone around.

'Listen, Ammajee. I am new here. Just come over on vacation for a fortnight or so. This is not my house. It is my friend's.'

She hears only the first part of what I say. 'I am new here too. Came just four or five days ago … to my son here … '

The above dialogue has been taking place all this while between two people—one standing in the balcony and the other in the room.

'Listen. Let me alert the neighbours. They belong here, know it inside out. They'll definitely help. And actually, it's not that late. Some last-minute work could have cropped up for your son.'

She murmurs. 'He could have at least told me that he'd be returning late.'

If he isn't to return at all? A doom-laden voice goes up within me and grips me. Who leaves word at the time of going? The time comes, sudden and without warning. And here are we poor humans closing our eyes to it, denying its omnipresence in our lust for living. It wouldn't let us live if we acknowledged it. It would cast its shadow ever and always, even as our greed and lust for life rage insatiably. Is this why we keep telling ourselves, we are, we too are, only *we* are?

'Let's go then, beti.' The old woman's anxious voice cuts into my soliloquies. I open the door. The landing is not dark, thanks to the light in the balcony. But the hush of the hills lies breathing on it, unshakable and immovable.

As soon as I see the full figure of the woman, I feel I've seen her many afternoons hanging out clothes for drying on the railing. A face torn and ridged by the ravages of age. Body thin and flat, dead-white hair, forehead covered and rimmed up to the brows by the *odhni* brought down low: on her body, a terylene salwar-kameez, discoloured by repeated washings.

I draped my shawl round myself, picked up my torch, and leading the old woman out, pressed the doorbell of the flat opposite. Time—a quarter past twelve to the dot—the first lap of the night.

The people who opened the door were definitely not ruffled. Nor did they look woken from sleep. Their clothes did seem in a bit of disarray though. And the man seemed to have got his kurta on the wrong side out. Both were clearly unwelcoming. Within seconds a cold film had spread over their faces, their eyes fogging over. And now they were in no frame of mind at all to see the things I wished to bring home to them and for which I had pressed their bell in the middle of the night.

'Forgive me for bothering you at this hour of the night. The fact is this old lady's son isn't back from the office yet, and she's worried.'

The man turned and looked at the clock on the wall, then at the dazed eyes of the old woman, and frowned: 'Nothing to worry, he'll come home. The President is in town these days. There's work in the office probably.'

'So late? Till this hour?'

'Why not? He's in the Maintenance Section after all.'

'But ... ' I wanted to say that the Maintenance Section was one thing, the President's visit another, but what I was talking about was something else altogether. There were of course, many other things possible—flood, earthquake, nuclear attack, terrorist attack, hail, fire—many things were possible in these valleys and these hilltops. But at this time, there was just this one thing, just these realities—a mother, her son, alien surroundings, midnight, danger, darkness—and the son not yet home.

'You are worrying for no reason. He's often late, this is not the first time. We've watched long enough. He hurt his forehead just the other day.'

It was the woman by the side of the man saying this. In a level, even voice, chewing her words between amused, faintly laughing lips.

'He was hurt? When was this? When?' The old lady's frail body rocked with worry and shock.

'Some days ago. Yelled the whole night. We gave him aspirin. In the morning he went to the hospital. They gave him tetanus shots there.'

'When was this? When?' The old lady clutched at the word 'when'.

'Some two months ago, I think. Who remembers?'

'He never tells me anything, see.'

I am shaken. The moment, and the urgency contained in it, a-flutter on the sharp tip of anxiety, are receding. Something is taking place somewhere, in some unknown realm of darkness. The old lady wants to tear apart and vanquish that unknown darkness, after having absorbed into her anxiety so many other darknesses.

'Get along, now, *maataajee*. Go to sleep. He'll come when he has to. It's work he has to do, not just dancing attendance on you.' The man speaks like a man.

'He needn't dance attendance on me. All right,' the old woman now retorts. 'But at least come back he should.'

Their dialogue was beginning to jar upon me. 'Isn't there anything we can do? Go up to his office or the police station? Offices close at five thirty, all said and done.'

'And who told you he'll be in the office?' the man said this in an undertone. The old woman, who was hard of hearing, definitely couldn't have heard him.

'If we go we can at least find out when he left office. We could make a quick round of the area too. You have a motor cycle.'

'No, no, it'll be a wild goose chase.' The man was decisive. He was making it clear that he wanted no more of this fuss.

'Then?'

'Then nothing. You people just go back to bed. Maataajee, I'm telling you, go back and go to sleep. He'll be home. If not, we'll see what next.' He made a faint sign to the woman beside him.

She went back into the house on firm swift feet and came out wrapped in her shawl. Circling the old woman's shoulders with her arm she got set to haul her out. 'Come. I'll take you home.'

I felt that the stone landing connecting the two flats on which we stood was beginning to shake, as though an earthquake was starting up within it. To keep the earth still what a lot we do! We build houses. Lay roads. Run trucks, tanks, tankers and trains on it, and yet the earth shakes. Shakes, because we fling away from this mountain of matter the binding energy of a vital emotion.

The old woman was being pushed. Pushed steadily along. An unseen yet noticeable pressure was being exerted by the hand circling her shoulders. It was violence that carried in it an alibi for its perpetrator, a violence able to be brought into action despite the overflowing distress of the old woman.

This yoking of strong violence to the stronger distress was unseemly, improper, immoral. And here I was, watching it all without moving a muscle.

Yes, it *was* I, watching it all, standing dumb, devoid of movement. I wondered who and what kind of people were those who could thwart midway the momentum of an attack, and thereby save a man on the brink of danger.

I was not one of them.

I was hurt that I was not.

In front of me was a sheet of windowpane. And stationed safe behind it I watched the old woman being dragged away.

The old woman dug her heels in, but was dragged along nevertheless.

The scene changed the moment the old woman vanished from the doorway of the couple. The air lightened.

The man was without his woman at his side. He turned his attention fully towards me now. He laughed openly and took it upon himself to explain things to me. In no time at all the tip of his finger rose to his right temple and circled it fast.

'She's got a screw loose here somewhere, don't you know. A thorough crackpot this old woman is. Lost her wits, she has. Puts the milk on the gas, the milk keeps boiling. Opens the tap, the water keeps running. Puts the roti on the *tawa*, it keeps cooking and chars. You know why? Because she's over there, back over there at Rawalpindi. Stupid she is, stupid, idiotic. Partition took place half a century ago, and she still has her ears cocked there. Just think, are forty-five/fifty years a small length of time? This is why I don't listen to her rubbish.'

'But right now, at this hour … '

'Forget the hour. Who'll keep sitting with her?'

My tongue is stuck to my throat. I want to say that the anxiety she is in at this moment would be evident even to a blind man. And who gives us the right, anyway, to dismiss a person's fears just because we are not part of that person's past? Who gives us the right to humiliate this woman, ridicule her, because we escaped being caught in the tunnel of the past? It was pure chance that we were on another piece of earth at that time. Geography saved us. And for that reason we stay indifferent forever?

'I know what you are thinking. That I am heartless …' The man broke into my line of thought. 'But this woman has weakened her case herself by harping on it day in and day out. She is stupid all right'.

'For this kind of stupidity there could be any number of reasons. Possibly, she lived in a kind of happiness over there in Rawalpindi which she's not been able to create here. If the aftermath is bearable, who cares for the over and done with?'

'God knows, this whole thing is beyond me. We have some refugees in our office too, all beat-up and washed up, impoverished from over there. But absolutely sane and fighting fit they are. Look, what had to happen, happened. Are you going to shed tears for it all your life?'

I was following another line of reasoning altogether. 'Between man and woman isn't there any difference at all? Look at the ways of release open to a man! But for a woman? And a woman of those times at that, far from being involved in any heroic attempts to change the world. Stays in the house, confined to its walls. Her sorrows too stay confined within her, never get worked out.'

'What kind of argument is this?' He curled his lip.

This man is far from keen to hear whatever I have to say or want to say—it is more than clear by now that he is just impatient to say his own say fast, stop beating round the bush. Or maybe he feels that without filling me in on his side of the affair he cannot count me as somebody within the ambit of his trust.

He goes on.'It's just some three or four years ago that her husband died. This old woman can't get over the shock of it. There's some irony there, I grant. A man lives through twelve hours of non-stop shelling in the Partition riots, only to die in his sleep years later lying next to her. But frankly I don't believe a word of what she says. She says the train that her man boarded to run out of Rawalpindi was stopped at Gujranwala station. There was a twelve-hour shelling, she says. The whole train was set on fire.'

'Was he alone?'

'Don't you know how it was? As soon as things began looking uncertain people sent away their families to India. The family heads stayed back to take care of property and business in whatever way they could, and see which way the wind blew. She says when the military came and soldiers entered each compartment of the corpse-laden train, and shouted that anyone left alive should come out, her man came out pushing off himself piles of dead bodies. As luck would have it, from the next compartment a labourer of theirs also came out alive. This fellow got room in a truck immediately and crossed the border into India, while her man was stranded, pushed and shoved around in camps. And finally he straggled over to Amritsar a month later. These people had given him up for dead. Oh, all right, they'd thought that, but he didn't die, did he? Why should this foolish old woman stay stuck in those happenings? Catches hold of anyone any time and launches forth.'

The man's flat accusing tones jarred upon me. Perhaps he read my distaste, and so said, 'You take her son now, her own son. He can't stand anything she says. You just ask him about these very things she goes on about non-stop, and he loses his temper. Growls, "All these age-old things, years and years old, when did I ever see them with my own eyes to think them true?" A very understanding boy he is basically, fully balanced.'

'How do you know all this?'

'O, this old woman has come to this town before, keeps coming.

Nags the boy day and night, all because he is alone.' Lines of contempt broke out on the man's face again. God knew why he thought himself empowered to play judge on the woman's life.

'Now look … he's a boy, young, single and free, why should he take on this nuisance? Is it easy managing this bundle of grief? But she turns up despite all his angry pleas not to, turns up to roll out his roties for him. Good god, will the boy not get his roties if she weren't around? He snaps at her all the time to go stay with his elder brother. He has a home, a regular household. There's a *bahu* there, grandchildren galore. Good or bad, they're there, far better equipped. But catch her listening! This kind of blind attachment is terrible, don't you agree?'

He now looks at me for confirmation. He has been patient with me on all counts. By his reckoning I should now in return endorse his views of things.

I have no answer.

I want to stay without answering. I have my own portfolio of beliefs. But I do not want to lay it open before this man. I do not want to tell just anyone who happens to be within earshot that all else might go, be swept away, but a mother stays intact, imperishable. Doesn't this signify eternity, timelessness, and not just a relationship? How is it possible otherwise, possible for this woman who breathes and bears the pain of history, to extend the shelter of her *anchal* to an unruly and uncouth son in the alien air of an alien city?

A man never knows the ever-giving nature of a mother's anchal. It can spread over even the dumb and voiceless, even over the inanimate things of nature. A woman knows this. A man does not, cannot. As protection against hail, tender fruit trees are covered with cloth, like a woman covering her child with her anchal. Hasn't this man living in this hill town seen this?

The woman who had gone with the old woman, the woman who is his companion, is now back. On her face is a smile of triumph. Not for no reason! It isn't any small feat she's pulled off—settling back in a dark poky room, a being born and bred in distant Rawalpindi! Knowing there is no electricity in that wing of the building! Rumour had had it that power would be coming there in three or four days, but many 'three or four days' had come and gone many times over without the promised light.

The woman is elated. She's narrating the story of her accomplishment. 'Know how the old woman was shivering? I've covered her with a blanket. She wouldn't sit, just wouldn't. I asked her what was the use of standing at other people's doorsteps? Stay put in your house, I said to her. He'd be back, I told her. As if he's not been late before!'

My head is reeling. The old woman huddled alone in the room, the thick darkness, the cot, the blanket, the shivering—and the homilies.

The man does not allow my attention to wander. 'All right, madam, now you too go off to sleep.' The tragi-comedy of the drama of Partition is over. Curtains down now. He claps his hands.

It is an end that seems abrupt. 'All right', that phrase of the man's sentence flutters in my mind, unvoiced.

Their door has closed.

I don't know when mine will.

Now?

I am suddenly left alone on the landing—unhappy and feeling drained. In the dim light of the landing a silence, equally dismal.

All this while, from end to end, within and without, there was noise. There was worry, pain, history, geography.

All this time those two were there. Then, there was only the man.

There was violence, anger, objection and analysis.

Now there is nothing. There is silence. Only I am. And with me is a clinging sense of guilt. It's an upsetting, unclean feeling. If nothing else, I can at least share the old woman's agony in the temporary lull of her immediate anxiety.

An unbearable something rises within me, propelling me towards the old woman's flat.

There is light in the balcony, and inside, pitch darkness. I don't have to knock on the door. It is unbolted.

I push open the door. In the thin ray of light that comes in, I see lying on the cot a crumpled, bundle-like object.

'Ammajee!' I call out in a low voice, switching on my torch.

'Who is it?' Ammajee starts and swiftly lights her own torch lying beside her .

'He hasn't come?' she turns her hollow, blank eyes at me.

'Must be on his way, would be in shortly.' I try to drill through the darkness with open, staring eyes. 'Come, let's go over there and sit ... in the light there. I am not sleepy yet.'

I thought she'd refuse, go stubborn, but no, in a trice she throws off her blanket and stands on the floor. Seeing her all set I begin looking around for the lock, by the glow of my torch.

She watches me fumbling about. 'What is it?'

'I'm looking for the lock.'

'Must be there on the small table. See how stupid I am? Keep forgetting. My memory has been gone god knows since when.'

'It is not so.' I admonish with full authority that voice enduring the punishment of not forgetting.

She does not hear, does not agree. She says, 'Ask anyone you like. Those people must have told you, haven't they?'

'Those people? Who are they? Which people? Rank outsiders! Why do you pay attention to them?'

'I have to. I have to live among them forever now.' It is a flat, toneless acceptance, like that of black people living in a prejudiced environment, calling themselves 'black'.

I lock the door myself. When I put my arm round her and draw her close to lead her out to my flat, a passion stirs, a current seems to run through me. This being enfolded in the curve of my arm, who is she? What is she? She is a very alive, very vibrant part of our history—compact.

I think she likes coming into the light. Likes also sitting cushioned in the sofa. Ensconced thus she runs her eyes all round, lids fluttering away, taking stock of the novelty round her.

'I'll go and make tea.' I don't ask her, just tell her. And steal a glance at the clock too. At this hour and minute of the clock, is her burden of worry a little lighter?

She seems to be shivering, though—seems to be biting down a fit of shivering.

'Are you cold?'

'No, not really … ' She begins tightening the wrap of her odhni round herself.

I take out a shawl from the cupboard and wrap it round her. She is embarrassed. 'Just look, clean forgot that I had to take a shawl when coming out. Didn't I tell you that my memory is gone? Those people are right.'

The affirmation is painful. To accept her loss of memory and wear it as a badge of identity, while the truth is that she stands firm in the vortex of memory! Outsiders are tugging at this sense of reality about herself she has deep down within her, stretching it this way and that. Small wonder she is going dotty!

I find myself sitting at her knees, on the ground. 'Listen to me, Ammajee, listen carefully. You have forgotten nothing. You remember too much, what you remember is too much. That is your real problem.'

'How?'

I am stuck. What I think and want to say is difficult to say in her idiom. How am I to say to her that time does not forgive those who do not forget, because such people get in its way, in time's way: time is always in a hurry to stay in the present every minute.

'How?' She repeats.

'Relax. I'll make the tea.'

When I bring the tea she is overcome. 'Do you know, Kaka's father also used to do this. When he couldn't sleep he drank spiced tea like this with *elaichi* and *laung*. He would wake me up too and make me drink it, no matter how fast asleep I was.'

Her eyes are still now, absolutely still. She seems to me to be entering the dark regions that the man in the flat had talked about. Even in the full light of the room, a different glow seems to be tinting and illuminating her face.

Looking at her I feel that we, the rest of us, are people sunk and buried in the garbage of time. Hers is the one face that shines even in the garbage, under a vow to rise above the filth, rebel against it.

It is good that at this moment she has gone somewhere far off from her fears for her son. But her fears have entered *my* mind. They are thumping away there as terror.

I sneak a glance at the clock. It is past two at night. Twenty minutes past. The hands of the clock seem to be racing ahead.

Caressing the cup in the hollow between her hands she is slurping the tea.

The first drops have hardly gone down her throat when she puts the cup down sharply, spilling the tea on the sofa.

'Listen, listen. That thud. It's his scooter. Kaka's back.'

She stands up with a jerk and walks towards the door. I rise with her to go on ahead and see, but step back. It is futile taking any kind of lead, I know it in my bones.

The din of the scooter rises, then fades, and fading more, sinks into the hills.

Fear grips me. The fear of a mishap deepens within me. The silence that lies spread between us seems fear-laden also.

I put the cup of tea back into her hands. But her dazed attention elsewhere stops her from accepting it.

I want some conversation going, some exchange that would release her from the silence coiled round her. But she seems sapped.

There is no glow on her face now. A sobbing desolation lies on it. In their sunken sockets are the small pits of her eyes clouded over—I seem to see her eyes properly this time.

Now her face looks fearful to me as if the spreading creases have soaked in its salts. From within me disappears too the image of her face of a few minutes ago, a face luminous with its straying into the antechambers of the past.

An ugly worry catches hold of me. If she loses her son in some fatal disaster, upon which spot on her back will she bear the blow and the load of its aftermath? Will she be relieved of her earlier blows a bit, to make room for the fresh blow? Or will she collapse under the weight now become double? Is any more power of endurance present anywhere in her frail body?

'How long is it since you came away from Pakistan?' I ask an unbelievably stupid question. I know it is no question, just the desire for conversation.

She doesn't answer. Despite the wraps round her she seems overcome by cold. On her face is a stubborn silence. A look as though she is not here, has gone somewhere else, somewhere beyond reach.

The clock strikes three. The hand has moved forward from its brief stop on the hour.

She is on her feet. I know this is no standing up, but acute restlessness. Flinging open the door she slumps against the frame.

Through the open door a strong gust of wind tears in, ten times stronger than her body.

'Staying inside would be better, Ammajee.'

'No.' It is a resounding 'no'. Her head resting against the frame of the door, she stands motionless. I stand behind her. Two pairs of feet, hers in front and mine behind, stay fixed at the door.

There's nothing more now. Only the rise and fall of our breaths in the ruts of consciousness. There is misgiving. There is a silence of many layers.

Suddenly, noise, noise too heavy for the silence, rises up the stairs.

Her son, reeling on the top step of the staircase, materialises on the landing. A strong whiff of liquor fills the air with his appearance.

He explodes, seeing the old lady standing at my door.

'You here? At this hour? Standing here at the house of outsiders?'

Forgetting her relief at seeing him she breaks out agitatedly and crossly, 'Couldn't you have told me you'd be late?'

'So what hit you, *I didn't tell you*? The skies came down on you? You come along straight now, back home.'

He throws me a look as though he'd hawk and spit at me. He takes custody of his mother's thin arm in his iron fist.

He moves ahead on the landing with fast, loping strides. Behind him, tottering and buckling, she is being dragged along.

five

Wait, Intezaar Hussain

This happened around the time Intezaar Hussain's *Bastee* was published. Straightaway he went to the book shop and bought a copy: and back home slipped the brand new book into the rack at the head of his bed.

Slipping it in, he counted the books in the rack again. *Bastee* was the tenth book to have come out so far on Partition. In these ten books lay enclosed an important stage of his life. He was sure he would feel a crying, compelling need for these books some day. Reading them he would be reading his own past, his own life.

But life, whether his own or others', moved on. And his crying need didn't arise. One day his wife said, 'Take these books away. The children need the rack.'

He stared hard at his wife. She told him to stop staring like that. She was not scared of him as she was in earlier days. Calamities had hardened her. Nothing scared her now.

He made an effort to put force into his retort. He did succeed in this, sometimes. How did the saying go—'one stroke of the blacksmith's equals one hundred of the goldsmith's'?

'I have said not once but many times that this rack will stay where it is, at the head of my bed. And these books too. Whoever moves it will move it over my dead body.'

It was the style of arguing he'd always called feminine: threatening suicide when words failed. Emotional blackmail.

And now *he* was the one speaking this language because he could not, in all honesty, think of a more clinching argument to shore up his refusal to empty the rack.

Her sagging cheeks shook in helpless rage. She didn't set much store by her husband's threat, but she couldn't laugh it away either.

She flung down the cardboard box she'd brought along for storing the books in, and called out in ringing tones to the children in their room. 'No rack, no nothing for you, you hear? Your grandfather has to have everything he fancies.'

The children were nowhere around. It was for him, he knew well enough; to show him up as a mean old man by weighing the pressing needs of the children against his whims. And he knew well enough too that the rack had to stay where it was, was not on any account to be moved from there. These books had to be near him, within reach. In the contents of these books the pulse of his life throbbed quietly. Some day he was sure to get the time for feeling this throb of the pulse. Some day, for sure, he would be sitting amidst the books, reading his past. No matter the day hadn't come so far. Given his strong longing for it, it was bound to come. And God forbid that they get taken out of sight and get buried in cellars.

His enraged wife didn't speak to him the whole evening. The next day too she stayed enraged, glowering. On a pile of things come up in a corner of the room after the whitewashing, she flung the children's books higgledy-piggledy. It was one more taunt aimed at him. She could have looked for another corner if she'd wanted to.

He decided not to take notice of it. And, getting smaller day by day, one fine morning the heap vanished. He didn't think it necessary to find out which other corner the children had found. As on all days he left for work at his furniture factory.

If ... If he had known that his wife's life span was so short, that she would die so soon, he would most certainly have given way. He would have spread out the books on a plank under his bed.

He did not know. Nobody does. Things meant to happen, happen, without so much as a by your leave. A sharp pain in the chest does not always augur death ... why then did she die? Slumped into his arms within the blinking of an eye, as if reproaching him, 'OK! Here you are, all yours now, children, rack, books, the whole caboodle, never shall I be butting in now!'

He swallowed his rage. Rage not so much over the squabble about the rack, as over a lot of other things. Her rank disloyalty at leaving him midway, for instance. Flare-ups and bickerings were the agreed terms of exchange in their life together, not this rude exit by one member.

The cold wind now cuts deeper into his rib cage. His heart too aches more. But why crib now about aches and pains?

Now there is no need to spread out the books on a plank under the bed. He himself has given up the room, made it over to the children, and set up camp on the plank bed in the front room. For the children he has bought a new rack. His, he has put at the head of his bed. Exactly as before, in anticipation of his dire need.

When she was alive it never crossed his mind that between life and books no relationship gets built. Books lie around because they have no link with life lived. No give and take, no incursion into each other's territory. If they did, would he have assembled just this handful of books on the carnage after the country's partition? Just ten book bearing witness to the massacre of lakhs! The Jews have proved cleverer, wiser, smelting their tragedy and sending it afloat into the arteries of the world. Was there no lion-heart in this country to describe this indescribable tragedy it had suffered?

No, he is thinking wrong; the correction comes on its own. Those who write are one class, and those uprooted another. The uprooted have no time for words, nor the nerve to feel in their palms the embers smouldering under their soles and study them. Look at his own self. For years the books have been calling him from the head of his bed, and he … he …

If he'd read these books, perhaps he'd have been free of their spell, his heaviness of heart lessened. He could have read them like fiction. They would have gone, gone clear out of his mind. Right now he doesn't even know what's in them. All he knows is that in them lies buried the balance sheet of his past and its mute pains.

Today …

This day again.

On the morning of Independence Day, sitting before the TV, he is feeling different, stirred beyond reckoning. This day comes every year—when he sees the screen as he would see happenings in other people's lives. But today. … Perhaps to certain events we are ever sensitive, with or without knowing. Perhaps it is like the dampness of roots down below that never dries up and ever courses. … Otherwise why would he stand head bowed, hands folded, springing from his chair on hearing the strains of the national anthem issuing from the screen? Alone in the room, he finds himself standing till the last, fading echoes of the refrain '*Jaya hé, Jaya hé, Jaya Jaya Jaya Jaya hé* … ' It happens to him involuntarily, like an instant that shakes awake the whole of destiny. You never come to know what, where, and which branch of the tree of memory is being shaken. Do our unguarded moments perhaps bring to our doorstep the saga of the past?

His granddaughter Sweetie comes into the room. The sky in the TV screen is awash with balloons painted the colours of the national flag, and he sinks within.

It is the fifteenth of August today, the fortieth year of the country's freedom. What a length of time, ah … hh … hhh! He re-sets time to his own speed and location. He was nineteen years old when he left Lahore, Nikkee's image etched in his mind indelibly, anchored there.

Now he is forty plus nineteen. That is, forty years past the freedom war. From then to now, forty plus nineteen, full fifty-nine. Fifty-nine years—a half-baked age, neither mid-field nor off to the boundary.

To see grandfather lost thus, to see him 'not there', makes Sweetie impatient. This is just the kind of thing that makes her flee her father. 'Papa is useless, grandpa', she complains. 'Never listens to me. Work, work, work—all the time, work': even today when it is a holiday for her, and he has to take her out to see the lights.

'The lights will be at night, child,' he reins in Sweetie's mounting impatience, bordering on rage.

'Not night. Evening,' she bridles.

'All right, evening. But evening's still a whole afternoon away, and anyway what's the point going with me? If I go, it'll be on foot … '

'I too will go on foot … '

But by evening it is peace between Sweetie and her papa. He'd known all along it would be so, that Sweetie would not go with her grandpa. That she'd go in the car with her father. And she wouldn't look grandpa in the eye, would look away, and say, 'It's like this, see, grandpa, why don't you also come with us … '

He laughs, so long and so much that tears flood his eyes. How would Sweetie know that he is not to go anywhere today? That he is to sit around the house alone! A something has been tapping for his attention for God knows how long now. He has to bring it close and see it, see it face to face. Surrender himself …

Everybody has gone. A hush lies all round, but the mind is not at peace. Why is it not? If there's silence without, and din within, how fearsome it seems! In a daze he sits down by the books. *Jhoota Sach* first? No. *Aag Ka Dariya*? No, not that either. … Then *Udas Naslein*?

No, this too, no. Finally he pulls out Intezaar Hussain's *Bastee.* A slim volume, easily held in the hand: its slimness decides him.

He knows well enough that a book is a book only till it remains in the rack, holding between its two covers long, horizontal lines. Once out of the rack it becomes something else, some other thing.

Intezaar Hussain had begun the book in the name of the city, swearing by it. But which city can this be? By what the book says, it is where the hero, Zakir, is in search of his first day in a new city of a new country. This kind of displacement puzzles him from the word go.

In God's name how could a new country come up on old soil … and in the new country a new city? How? And in this 'new city' yet to come, a stranger, an unknown citizen, is looking for his first day in it: the first sacred day bathed in the sacred fire of freedom.

For the life of him he cannot make up his mind whether to laugh or cry at this irony of a search for a new country on old land. Wasn't the sacredness of the fire of freedom the only radiance for lighting up the soul? Otherwise it is the same on both sides of the line: the same gloom, foreboding and grief he has never forgotten: the very same gloom, foreboding and grief which Intezaar Hussain is dwelling on. On each succeeding page a shadowy nervous agitation quivers. A lot is being said, but nothing is clear. On every other page are accounts of trickery, police firing, of curfews in the offing: of heated debates in coffee houses about 'agents of imperialism' and 'mongrels of compromise'. Nothing but straws in the wind and motes of dust heralding a major catastrophe brush his understanding as he turns the pages.

He loses heart, feels outside it all even while stationed dead centre in a circle of flames.

His unhappiness grows. No! None of this is what he had been wanting to, waiting to, read. But … but … wanting to, waiting to, read *what*? He cannot tell. Which part of the past is he so avid to touch?

In great agitation he turns the pages fast, feverishly. So far he hasn't even got the name of the city where the hero is drifting about. Roads, turnings and by-lanes appear but without names. Nothing to identify them. Not that he does not know the names of the cities! Flashing forth in his mind as if by the wave of a wand, the names of the cities would not have changed so soon.

So far, the hero's loafing around is all that he has gleaned, but abruptly there intrudes a name he knows so very well. *Anaarkali Bazaar.* He reads: 'Anaarkali Bazaar—partly open, partly closed. A heavy crowd but no big buyers … '

The bare name 'Anaarkali Bazaar' stops him in his tracks. Aah..!. Now at last Intezaar is identifying the city. He sits up, feeling the need to sit up. This, yes this, is his own city! Wait a while, Intezaar Hussain …

The narrative ahead, he feels, is about to take a turn to Mall Road. You must halt, Intezaar. Let me get my breath back

But perhaps in Intezaar Hussain's hand the text of the novel is tugging at its reins. It is raring to break into a canter. He stops on his own. Pausing long and repeatedly to read the passages twice over, thrice over. Sitting on this side of the border now, he is reading the face of his city there, on that side. Rapt. Swallowing the lumps rising in this throat.

Now a new eye opens in him. He walks in step with the hero. 'The hero', Intezaaar Hussain writes, 'is relishing his walk in the new country. From the first road to the second, from the second to the third … ' God knows how long he keeps pace with the hero. It is after ages, after countless numbers of years that he is walking there free, free of the nagging fear that somebody edging past would stick a knife into him.

He is reading about the caravans of refugees entering the city, and his mind is in a turmoil. He … among the myriads forced out of Lahore. If it is Walton Camp this side, it is the D.A.V College Camp that side.

Moving with Intezaar's text he advances farther. 'In Sham Nagar so many houses stood empty. Doors and windows wide open, whole sets of furnishings were visible through the open windows. It looked as if the people going away just rose to their feet, picked up some clothes and stepped out.'

Ahh … h … h! How did you know all this, Intezaar Hussain? But you should have known, still, that it was not Sham Nagar. It was Sant Nagar. Sant Nagar … his home, his locality.

The evening hadn't waned yet. Father came in fast and halted dead centre in the yard. Heavy lines of tension were on his forehead and he stood with arms akimbo. Eyes fixed on the tongues of flames darting in the *choolah*. A cooking vessel was on it.

A knob of ginger in her hand, Mother came in. He said, 'Take down that vessel.'

'Whatever for? The dal's hardly done yet.'

'Just take it down!' No temper rang in his voice but what rang was nothing sweet either.

Seeing his mood, Mother held the vessel with the ends of a dishcloth and brought it down. Father turned, filled the bucket at the hand pump and poured a thick jet of water on the fire. The flames died. The choolah slumped under the black slurry of ash and soot.

'Now listen. And pay attention … those people have come. At the head of the lane they are now. Hurry and look sharp. We must go this minute.'

'Where?'

'To the camp. The D.A.V College camp. The government promises no safety to those sticking it out in houses. We will have to stay there for now. Hurry. Just shove in some clothes … '

Into a long canvas bag he was squeezing in a blanket.

His unmistakable fluster now had its effect on Mother. Scared, she said, 'Clothes, yes. But upstairs all the windows and doors are wide open.'

'O forget about doors and windows, woman. Get out double quick. Have you no idea ... ' He leaned across to whisper into her ear.

'Wait, Father. I'll go close the doors and windows ... '

He darted towards the staircase, but how could he have the wits left to close the doors and windows of the floor above? His thoughts were riveted upon Nikkee, on warning her, reaching the terrace where he had his hush-hush trysts with her.

Living one house away from his, every time Nikkee's face came into view he knew he had to go up. To the terrace. At once. By any means. Go up and gratify her naughty demands. Standing in the closed stairway down the back of the house, Nikkee would be waiting for him. He had to go to her and crush her in his arms. Crush her so hard, so hard, that ...

He remembered how once, under the pressure of his maddened embrace, a scream had escaped her. In a panic that her brother Kirpal would be somewhere around, he clamped his hand on her mouth. So hard that she backed away and tumbled down a couple of steps. Her back got bruised, of course, but her knee was hurt too. A swelling came up at the joint.

'Roshan, you've gone crazy for sure today. What'll I tell them below?' She was scared.

'O come on. Tell them anything. Excellent fibber that you are ... '

That evening he learnt from his mother that Chawla Saheb's daughter, Nikkee, had had a fall in school. That her back had been bruised, that a nagging pain in the knee had set in. A nagging pain, his mother said was nasty, goes on and on. He also learnt that later in the evening his mother would be going to Nikkee's to ask how she was.

His generous offer to close the doors and windows—he clean forgot on the very first step. He wanted to clear the stairs in one bound. And alert Nikkee of what he'd heard his father say about the *balvais*—the rioters. Alert her. His mind drummed Nikkee … Nikkee … Nikkee … Nikkee wouldn't half know the things his father knew … that they had come in, were breaking into houses.

Hauling the menfolk out, tying them to trees, butchering them. And under their very eyes, stripping their women … . oh … h … h!. His breath came in gasps.

The moment he set foot on the terrace he felt stark terror. From down below rushed up a torrent of screams and pleas. Perhaps they had come up to Nikkee's house. A balvai stood guard on the top step of the stairway from Nikkee's terrace. He still remembers the eyes of that brute—like live, burning coals, and the tight black band round his jaw …

As Roshan advanced, a stentorian voice went up. 'You there! Twerp! Freeze … I'll take care of you, else … ' Without moving he aimed the glinting tip of his spear at Roshan.

He does not now remember when his father came up to the terrace in search of him. When he gave him a kick on his back with the flat of his sole. When he dragged him all the way down the stairs. He remembers his father's hard, vice-like grip round his wrist, and ringing in his ears, Nikkee's rising scream. A scream like that of an animal not yet dead, into whose entrails a maniac pushes in and pulls out a serrated knife. Pulls, keeps pulling …

Pain floods him. Forty plus nineteen years later. He breaks down. Crumbles.

Drilling through the hard crust of massed ice he cried. Sobbed. Sobbed unceasingly as if a scream condensed in the breast of time had suddenly started melting; dripping like blood, drop by drop.

All this happening now. After all these years. To an old man of nineteen plus forty years who had resolved then, forty years ago, 'This is a war for freedom. Over this war none of us is ever to cry. For any loss. At any time'.

six

Yatra

There, there it goes up again—that voice—

'Kittoo … Kittuaa … !'

Emerging from the heart of the *haveli*, it bounds out to the rear, faint but edged with authority. It's ten in the night: gets late coming back home from the hospital via the bazaar for all the buying and shopping. As for settling down with the books, it is a distant idea as yet, flapping around in the corners of his head.

'Kittoo … .Kittuaaa … '

That maiming of his name makes him see red. If not 'Kishan' couldn't it at least be 'Kishna' or 'Kishnoo'! But whose plaint gets anyone anywhere in this regime? Go grumbling to Bapu, and you get the stock answer: 'What difference does it make? Born to rule, they are. Can call you anything!'

Why? Why doesn't it make a difference? Your own name thrown back at you mauled and misshapen and it shouldn't make a difference? On his high school certificate is written 'Krishanchandra'. That's his name too. He reads it, and he feels that it clothes an unclothed body, adorns it. He moves his hand again and again over the letters of that name. The letters stay flat on their backs, stay just as they are. But within him something rises, like the level of water.

'What do I put down after it, Bapu?' he'd asked his father once, he recalls, drowning in the recollection.

'What do you mean, "what after it"' ?

'I mean surname, the name after the first name. Don't you understand? I mean, what is our caste name?'

'Who do you think you are—a princeling or something? "What is our caste!"' His father aped him. 'Gone bloated with getting your fill here, haven't you, scrounger!'

Bapu himself was a killjoy of the first order. Why blame others?

The voice rends the stillness again. A special rasping tone saws through it now. And here he was, thinking of forgetting about food and eating, just getting down to the business of studying. Food brings on drowsiness. But nothing can be done now. That voice is not to be ignored. When it is heard, it is demanded of him, demanded of the composition of his blood that he run, run like a sprinter over the white line of chalk.

He goes in. The job is trite. Tarun Babu has suddenly found the sheets on his bed dirty, and wants them changed. Right away, pronto. So what if the sheets were changed every Saturday? So what if it is only Thursday yet?

Tarun Babu doesn't let go any chance now. Waits with narrowed eyes, working out ways and means of destroying by the roots the standing that has come to him, the lowly Kituaa, a boy his own age: a standing that has overshot his own standing as the one born to rule. He enjoys this game to the hilt—this game of calling him over, and feasting his eyes on his stance of the ready slave. His father is bed-ridden. And he's helped himself to the right of getting obeisance.

Silently he changes the sheets, making himself blind to Tarun Babu's presence. He's about to leave, through with the task, when the harsh voice rings out: 'Wait. Sit down.'

Sit where? At his feet? At a point most respectfully off the corner of the rug? There's no other place in the room.

'Haven't you heard? I said sit.'

A no-nonsense tone crackles in the voice. He hitches up his pyjamas and sits.

'From this stack of newspapers here under this table take out all the photos of Kapil Dev batting. For my album.'

Work of this kind? The full load of studies is waiting for him. The hour of the night oppresses. Hunger and thirst gnaw. Yawns pile up and stiffen him, but his body is trained to disregard its own signals.

He picks out the photos. But to Tarun Babu they seem lacking somewhere. He wants text and narration along with action. 'Narration, narration. Don't you know what narration is? The big scholar that you are!'

Precisely where this iron nail is being hammered in, he knows, knows without having to raise his eyes. He knows about the nerve throbbing within Tarun Babu, throbbing without let-up. All this wealth and show are his, this nerve throbs. Power and prerogative are showered upon him by fortune. But why don't achievement and success follow suit? Why does this Kitua go up step by step and he … he the heir to this vast estate, he … !

When he stands up he sees that Tarun Babu has stretched out his legs upon the table, and screened his face with a newspaper, like screening off from sight things not fit to be seen. Anger seethes within him.

Back in his room, his decision to study vanishes. Hunger leaps at him. Should he hold back hunger with the whip of will and sit down to study? No, at this moment, he is robbed of even this familiar discipline. What is he to do with books and studies? They take you deeper and deeper down roads to a futureless void. Far better it would have been if he'd flung these books away as bricks and stones of no use, flung them as far as he could. It is these books that have messed up his life, left him as neither fish nor fowl. How good it would have been if he too, like Bapu …

The haveli had seen Bapu in his boyhood. It had seen him in his youth. And now it was seeing him in his tottering middle age. Bapu's boyhood had been spent tagging behind mother, tripping all over these floors. His dreams hadn't gone beyond, not beyond trotting behind his mother and making it to adulthood: not gone beyond learning the sacred rituals of serving and attendance, unlacing the boots of his master when he got back from court, filling his pot with water for his ablutions. Not beyond thinking up newer and ever more creative ways of dancing attendance: making his ministrations so silken smooth as to compel his master to raise his eyes and look.

In the eighth class his son stood first, and Tarun Babu failed. Pepped up by the glances of encouragement and smiles of affection from the *Maalkin,* he was casting about for going up to her, when Bapu froze him with one single look, immobilising him right there at the threshold of the room. Placing the maalkin's betel-leaf box on her bed, Bapu bounded over to him, dragged him back to his quarters, and pushed him in.

'There's no need for you to go there. It's no great feat you've pulled off, all right? Don't you know Tarun Babu's results? How do you think the Maalkin is feeling about it?"

He wilted. He was new here yet. He couldn't make out why Bapu's own joy had to be curbed because of gloom in the haveli.

No such questions bothered Bapu. He could without effort throw away as unnecessary for himself too whatever part of him was not needed by the haveli.

How strange. Even after marriage Bapu never felt any great urge to set up home in the village, to be with wife and children. He just left mother in the village. Once a week or once in ten days he'd pay a visit. At times he even lingered, but as dusk fell, he'd be on tenterhooks to go back to the city, as though his real home was there.

From the village Mother sometimes insisted on coming to the haveli. His father's chronic absence had given untimely weight to his still young years. He'd put on a stiff new shirt, fix a round, embroidered cap on his head and trot along to the bus depot with his mother.

Bapu would flare up at the very sight of them. 'Couldn't stay put there? Coming up here to stuff yourselves with free food! What do you think this is, an eating house? Couldn't you have come after eating there?'

It hurt him. He'd get ready to tell him that they had, indeed, come after eating. But Mother, sitting beside him and hidden behind her *ghoonghat*, would pinch him hard on his thigh, meaning hush up. She'd tell him later, when they were back in the village, that at least on the pretext of eating they'd been able to spend some time there.

Bapu would go up to the maalkin sheepishly, and tell her, one foot across the threshold, the other still outside, 'Those folks of mine have turned up. Just landed up. What are they to eat?'

The maalkin would break out laughing. 'Well, go ahead and feed them! Observe the courtesies!'

But Bapu would be growling and snapping. In a blackened pot he'd cook rice with salt. For himself, he'd pop a lump of *gur* into his mouth and wash it down with water.

'Why are you doing this? What's lacking here?' Mother would frown.

'And so we eat up everything? Because there's nothing lacking?' Bapu's thought patterns were forever slanted in favour of the haveli.

On Mother's death he saw for the first time Bapu stay at home for many days running. Outside was the hazy light of dusk. In the sky the bilious yellow mass of an impending storm. Outside the hut lay his dying Mother, stretched flat on the ground, head covered with the *palloo* of her sari stretched tight below the eyes. Her breathing was hard, laboured. A little away, sitting propped against the wall, Bapu was desperately intoning, 'Siri Ram, Siri Ram.'

'Just give me a hand, will you, Laalaa?' He still remembers the sharp note of irritation in his elder aunt's voice as she called out to Bapu.

Bapu came over. But his hands were limp, not conditioned to this task. He stood around fumbling. Only after she breathed her last did his hand go up to her forehead. He clasped his fingers round her wrist once, and silently, put her hand down again.

When Mother's last rites were over, he was face to face with his father. So far Mother had been his lee. Sheltered by it he could gaze at his father with detached curiosity. The lee was gone now. Everything was torn apart, exposed, it seemed. He was not ready for a one-to-one meeting with his father. And not ready at all for this question from Bapu:

'And so, son, where will you live now?'

'I … I … ' Standing under a sky that seemed endless and shoreless he suddenly broke down crying.

Bapu thawed. 'I was just asking if you'd be staying in the village or in the city.'

What could he answer? If he stayed in the village where would he stay? If he went to the city where would he go? For Bapu these problems didn't exist. His life was an even flow that quickened pace and swirled deep when it ran along the walls of the haveli.

Bapu arranged his son's life too in his own way. He made a proper distribution of everything—cooking vessels, clothes, pots and pans, spoons, sieves—and landed in the haveli, along with him. His head was bent low, as if he expected the haveli's foundations to shake with the weight of his good-for-nothing son.

He was blissfully easy in the mind about him after bringing him over. His duties were done. Installing him this close, he had no eye left for him. Didn't he ever think what he was to do amidst these quadrangles and walls and courtyards? Here there was neither Santu nor Jaggi, neither field nor well, neither plain nor pond. He couldn't scuff his feet around here. There was no snatch and grab for *singharas*, no joy of stealing sugarcane from the fields at night. Here there was just a shed of a room beside a porch way, and Bapu, who wished that Kishna wouldn't stay in sight when the master returned from court, wished that he'd just evaporate. Tarun Babu was his peer, age-wise, perhaps two years older. When he saw him first he was excited, but soon understood that this equality of age was just something for the record, to be noted from a distance. It was a strong, ruthless wall. His examination results made him more of an outsider than ever.

There was just the maalkin, a stark exception to all this. Seated on the dazzling white sheet of her divan, clad in a fresh, starched sari, she'd be arranging cones of betel leaves on a plate. Her bangles slid up and down her arms, making their own music. Her face glowed.

Emerging from his shed he'd stop shyly at her threshold.

'Well, little one, why do you stand there? Come along in.'

He'd slither in on slow feet, clinging to the wall. That kind of invitation couldn't be turned down.

'Don't you speak yet?'

He'd go more awkward. From the soft flesh of her upper arm he'd turn his eyes away. Her face glowing in the glow of her red sari ... He'd go tongue-tied.

Back in the village, there had been his mother, dried of body, wasting away day by day. This beautiful lady could never have seen his mother properly. If she had she'd definitely have done something. After all it was her good offices that had given him admission in the government school.

Bapu could not understand why he was hovering around her room on the day his examination results came out. He'd pushed him back into his quarters after a round of scolding. But he couldn't stay in there. To be thus dismissed and declared a no-good fellow was hard to take at this particular time: so many red lines of excellence shone on the yellow paper of his report card!

The maalkin was assembling the items for the evening *pooja*, seated before the altarpiece carved into the almirah. She was dipping cotton wicks in ghee. Her face was not smiling, he noted. He was afraid at first.

'Come in, boy,' a sad voice called him in. 'Come in … here, take this.' Her closed fist opened into his. 'You've stood first in class I hear! Go have your fill of *jalebis*.'

A light suffused his face. On an impulse he bent down and touched the maalkin's feet. She was overcome. 'Run along now. Be happy, very happy … ' The sound of her deep sigh followed him all the way out of the room.

Outside, he opened his fist. A crumpled two-rupee note lay in it. A wave of an emotion unknown surged through him. This reward was for him … him! Without any mediation from Bapu, it had come straight from the maalkin. Bapu would be lost for words, seeing this. He would keep awake till Bapu came, wouldn't go out even for eating jalebis.

Bapu came, worry creasing his face. Maalik had given a thrashing to Tarun Babu for failing in the tenth class. He had compared the two of them, openly proclaiming the different futures that awaited them, the lines of which were already there to see. 'He is better than you in every way … far better: reads by the light of a lantern but stands first.'

'Then go adopt him!' Staring at the maalik with bold, impudent eyes Tarun Babu stomped up to the terrace. The maalik was wounded, inside and outside. Sorrow, despair, rage, anxiety … what was not worrying him?

Bapu came in loaded with just these worries. He had by now got used to this trait of Bapu's. Bapu laughed with the haveli, cried with the haveli, exulted and despaired with the exultation and despair of the haveli.

Bapu took off his kurta, hung it on a nail, and stretched out on the charpai—not having his gur and water. This break in his routine …

Leaning against the wall, he sat on the ground, waiting for Bapu's attention. But Bapu's face and eyes were far away. No, he couldn't wait any longer.

'Bapu! Look!'

'What is it?'

'Take a look, Bapu. It's from the maalkin, for standing first.' Suddenly going wordless and stammering, he fluttered the note before Bapu's eyes.

Bapu sat up with a jerk. 'What? The maalkin gave it?'

'That's right! The maalkin gave it. Called me in herself. "Buy jalebis for yourself", she said.'

Bapu's face came back fully from wherever it was. He saw his son straight and solid, took full note of his presence before him. Usually, by now …

Bapu drew him close. Moving over his head, his hand slid down the back of his neck, came to rest on his shoulder. It was a totally new sensation for him, totally unfamiliar, without precedent in his life so far. He was shaken.

Bapu folded him in his arms. 'You see for yourself, don't you, how upset the master is from Tarun Babu's goings-on? Why does a man rear offspring, after all … '

Bapu was lost again. The mere reference to offspring and why a man needs one transported him back to the haveli.

The abrupt slackening of Bapu's embrace hurt enormously. But he consoled himself with the still-present warmth of his touch. In the total happiness of that moment he forgot Bapu's wandering attention. He folded that touch like a precious cloth and tucked it away within him. No, he would never make Bapu suffer such anguish. He would never make him a father driven to putting a question mark over the aim and import of bringing forth offspring.

Tossed by such thoughts he couldn't sleep till late in the night. He was still asleep even when the day had advanced far. He would have slept more if Bapu hadn't woken him up, looking deeply and fondly into his face. 'You'll get late for school, Kishna, my child.'

Such fondling and caressing … and from Bapu! He closed his eyes and bathed in the waves of the pleasure.

'I've arranged for a bottle of milk for you daily. Aren't you in a higher class now? With more to study? Come, get up. I have to go. The master is up already.'

This bridge was new. Despite its two opposing ends it arched and met like a bow. He couldn't really fathom what it was that was feeling so new, so good.

Just as he couldn't fathom what this other thing was, how it had come about. But it had. Between him and Tarun Babu a rivalry smouldered. Where there was no relationship, an oblique, crooked and besmirched relationship began to form. There was no comparison between them, couldn't be. Tarun Babu studied in a British-style elite school, he went to a government school. The car took Tarun Babu and brought him back, he trudged in the burning sun. Tutors came to Tarun Babu's house to bring him up to scratch. He wore his eyes out, peering into his books in the smoky light of the lantern. No, there was no area where they stood shoulder to shoulder, nothing that made the scales of judgment tip in his favour.

In his tussles in the haveli, he kept a low profile. Nonetheless a cold, cruel glee ran in his veins sometimes, beyond the reach and understanding of Tarun Babu. If Bapu got wind of it he'd flog the life out of him, tear him out of his senses. So he steeled himself to take things with a stolid face. He put everything into his studies. He knew there was no other way he could knock down Tarun Babu, checkmate him well and proper. He just had to keep climbing the mountain of attainments with single mind and absolute devotion, and once on top, stand there chest out, leaving himself open for others to gaze at.

In the tenth class he got a first division again. The school presented him a shining trophy as the best all-rounder. It gave him a scholarship too for the next two years. And as always, Tarun Babu's marks had to be hiked up by behind-the-scenes efforts.

Bapu got scared, leave alone being overcome with joy. Stammering for words, he snatched the trophy from his hands and thrust it under the pile of quilts.

'Why, Bapu?' He cried out, cut up.

'Let it be, let it lie there.'

'Why Bapu, why?'

Bapu's face looked like sunlight withdrawing from a valley. 'No, son, none of all this will be tolerated by anyone,' he said and strode towards the haveli on swift feet. He was left standing in the darkness of the shed, hurt, alone.

Bapu didn't get back even to give him his food. Perhaps he was avoiding him. He sent the maid to him with his food.

That evening, all by himself, the boy sat under the *pipal* tree, threw stones at the wheel of the well near by, and made faces at the monkeys. He wasn't interested even in showing his cup to the maalkin. It just stayed under the stack of quilts.

Why didn't Bapu understand that these extreme scruples of his didn't mean a thing?

Disgust deepened within him. Bapu's peace, acquired by strangling his own son's desires, had left such deep scars on his son's neck that they smarted always. What Bapu wanted to erase and deny broke out more into sight. What he wanted to wipe out became more entrenched, put down roots farther below.

What exactly was Bapu scared of? Was he scared of the grace, the *punya*, earned by him from his severe austerities to eliminate himself, make himself devoid of rights? Rooted for centuries in the black mud of servility, was he scared of this faint glow of brightness in his being? Didn't he have the strength to take even this small right accruing to him? Why did he want to draw into the depths of degradation his very legs that held him up?

No, this could not go on. Tonight he would speak fully and frankly to Bapu. He would make him see everything he did not wish to see. Into his crippled legs he would pour strength. Holding him by the arm he would take him beyond the yard of this house, beyond the reek of his sick being.

He waited, waited. Bapu came late. He put up the flame of the lantern the moment he came in, to show him that he was still awake.

Bapu stared hard but said nothing. Without taking off his shirt he sat down pressed against the wall, wiping his sweat.

'What's the matter, Bapu?'

'Nothing. Changing the tyre has drained me. Tarun Babu … '

'Why, were you out with Tarun Babu?' He tore through Bapu's hedging.

'There's a party for his friends tomorrow. He's passed his exams, you know! Had to buy things.'

'You like doing all this, Bapu?'

He was sure he'd say yes, exult in his loyalty to his masters. But he was quiet. Tired and hurt.

This sudden vulnerable but reachable state of Bapu, defences down, was just too good to let go. 'Tell me, Bapu,' he coaxed.

'What's left to tell … at this fag end of my life … why shed tears now … '

'Let's go away somewhere, Bapu, why not?'

For a while Bapu studied him, eyes still lost, far away. 'No, son. He is a heart patient. How can I leave him now?'

'Does anybody else care that he's a heart patient?'

'That's just why! If Tarun Babu had been different … '

'Are you under contract to him? If … '

If all he wanted was servitude he could get plenty of it anywhere for the asking. The words fluttered on his tongue but he bit them back. Their lash wouldn't have fallen anywhere else, but on Bapu's mystique, on the purity embedded under the skin of his servitude.

'It's okay breaking your back for your master, Bapu, but Tarun Babu? Just think, he has no respect for even age.'

Silence. Stretched full on the length of the *charpai*, Bapu was moaning.

He felt, he didn't know why, that it was his own arrested childhood that had thrown Bapu into this pit of fire. The haveli was no more like a cool flowing river, seated on the bank of which everyone could draw in his share of coolness. Red embers were crackling in its foundation now. And here was Bapu attached to these very foundations, not the walls: in perpetual dread of the events that could rock the foundations. And there was Tarun Babu, stoking embers at these very foundations with both hands. Nothing could be done now, except for taking away Bapu.

The previous night the master had had a heart attack. There was no provocation from any quarter at the time, no reason for the unmistakable ache. First they thought it was indigestion, but when powders, packs of *heeng* and poultices of turpentine didn't help, the doctor treated him for the heart. Bapu was drained, broken. This is even more disturbing. Grief is gnawing at his heart. 'Three months' rest,' the doctor said.

Tarun Babu felt suffocated in the house, as if his wings had been clipped. Father bedridden, unending streams of visitors, papers to sign—he got his excuse for dumping studies. He didn't waste any time bringing it home to the visitors that grateful as he was for their concern he would have to learn to live without it. He had a host of other things to attend to … etc., etc.

Thus, he appropriated the evenings for himself, hitherto the hours for social visits by all and sundry, and began utilising them for wild jamborees with cronies.

Bapu wouldn't stir from the haveli. As if tied to its four sides, he hovered round the master. And he bore with composure, all through the day, the maalkin's unfamiliar face of hushed grief. But as soon as he stepped into his quarters, he released the full force of his despair upon his son. The echoes of his laments hovered around the walls till the next morning.

'In pain a man lies flat on his back! But the master? There's no pain in his body. It's his mind that's wounded. His mind, understand, son? And on top of it there's Tarun Babu. Just gone and barred all guests and visitors. They would have kept up the master's spirits … '

He was in none too good a mood himself. Mangal, the driver, had told him that the night before Bapu had coaxed Tarun Babu away from his cronies and attempted with reason, persuasion, cajolery and a hundred other means to make him abandon his wild ways, and Tarun Babu had sprung at him in attack. If Mangal hadn't intervened …

He had no interest whatsoever in these worry beads for the master that Bapu wore round his neck, no interest whatsoever. His interest lay only in Bapu, in making Bapu come to his senses, and this task seemed to be getting more complex by the hour. He made no response to what Bapu said.

Not getting a response Bapu took the subject no farther. He gave himself over to the charpai.

And he, cut up as he was himself, paid no attention to Bapu. In the light of the lantern he kept up his pretence of reading.

Glug-glug—Bapu poured water from the *surahi*. After drinking he stayed squatting near it. This pointless sitting and shuffling around distracted him.

'You could have asked me to pour it for you,' he said, puncturing the silence.

Bapu stayed mute. Then he got up and lay down, eyes open. Stark hopelessness shrouded his face.

He softened, he didn't know why. Who was bickering with whom and why?

'Want me to press your feet, Bapu?' He wanted to convey to him his presence and being. Not waiting for an answer, he placed his hands on his calves.

'No … ' A very weak 'no' rose from Bapu, and he went slack.

But for the first time he felt that he had been able to reach Bapu with the touch, touch the peace and ease that flowed with the flow of his blood, touch it deeply. He felt that he was able to reach Bapu straight and direct. And Bapu too was surrendering himself—giving himself over to him, his son.

From then on something began forming in his mind. He took over fully the sweat and toil of Bapu's duties in the haveli. He didn't stay in the Maalik's room in day-long vigil like Bapu. But he was not inattentive either. Buying the fruits, vegetables and medicines, fetching the doctor—all this he took up without being told, and saved Bapu the donkey work. He hated the sight of his father slogging, trudging in the hot sun, one foot in the house, the other in the bazaar. It felt good now, seeing his father basking in the ease, drinking it in drop by drop through each pore.

God alone knew what had been driving Bapu all this while! Had some wild beast driven its horns into his ribs? But he too could now see the cracks in the haveli. The master flat on his bed, the maalkin consumed by worry, Tarun Babu prowling around like a bully. A minute's delay and he rained abuses on all and sundry, blind to the claims of loyalty, to the demands of plain decency.

Now his Bapu's feet made for his own quarters again and again, wanting to see his son sitting and reading by the lantern, head bent, charting out his future with his own efforts. If the son put a little fruit or sweet into his hand, he'd stare. 'When did you go to the market?' … 'Why did you go?' … 'Don't you know that whenever you are away this whole place seethes with unrest?' 'How do you keep pace with things, son? How do you manage it?'

When Bapu lay at night with limbs stretched, his hands clasped his calves, and gently massaged them. In the beginning Bapu refused his services, true to his nature. These were services he rendered for others, never received them in return. Now he stayed quiet. He fell asleep, feeling the waves of pain ebb in the flesh between his calves and his son's hands. In the dead of night his eyes would snap open, piercing the dark.

The whole mass of his past condensed into a hard lump and sank into his breast. What had he done in all the years he'd been given? Watched his life fade away. Kishna's mother died starving. He'd tended her neither in body nor spirit. Three abortions she'd had, expelled half formed lives from within her. And he never woke to the events around him. What could she have been doing or thinking before she died?

Things long past and over come up flapping and rip through him like scissors. What had he done till now? When his head bent down at the threshold of the master, it had stayed bent. That was all right, he had no regrets about that. But apart from the threshold and his bent head there was also a heavy beam above. Why hadn't he ever seen the beam? Why?

The moment he saw the maid's boy at the doorstep he smelt danger. The boy sat there, casual and indifferent, his long shirt covering bare, knicker-less legs. In the house, Bapu tossed in pain. Carrying a full bucket of water in the afternoon he'd slipped on the slime by the well. Turmeric paste, fomentation, oil massage—nothing helped. He took him to the hospital. They admitted him straightaway. It was urgent. A bone in the right thigh had broken, and the left knee had cracked. An operation could well be necessary, the doctor said, but would be confirmed only after the plaster was removed.

For a day or two Bapu's absence rocked the haveli. By now every brick and tile of the building had got used to his hands. But very soon Bapu's duties were made over to him. That was bound to be, he knew. But unlike Bapu, he refused to make himself available any and every moment of the day. He stuck to his quarters, came over when called. He didn't bother too much to hide his displeasure if called away from work he valued more than the mean, fetching and carrying jobs he was put to in the haveli. The maalkin turned a blind eye to it all. But for him there was no respite from Tarun Babu. He, Kishna, now stood face to face with him—he was the nemesis who could, even as an underling, show up his master's incapacity as not only high but superlative.

Leaving for the hospital he was all clouded over inside. Smouldering within him was the heat of the violence stirred up in the tussle over the photos of Kapil Dev. If he hadn't wasted all those hours last night on that silly job he'd have got still more marks in the test. Nearing the hospital his heartburn flared up afresh. The very thought of Bapu, the haveli and the whole set-up raised his hackles. With Bapu hospitalised and out of the way, he had the power now to fully wrest eye for eye and tooth for tooth for the violence that raged in the haveli. But his banal avenger's exultation wavered at the sight of Bapu's face. He seemed extraordinarily full of spirits today. For the past two days he had lain inert, semi-conscious, rocked by the pain of the bones settling back in place.

'Listen, son ... ' He was beside himself with excitement. 'See that patient over there on bed number four? He's got a case pending in the court for the last three years. I told him that my son would help him out and straighten all his papers ... '

Bapu spoke as though he was not a student but a lawyer, and had the power to dispense justice.

Such a glow of pride there was on his face that all his tension vanished. He sat on the stool, relishing the two-way gaze of Bapu's eyes. One was on him, the other on the effect of his presence on others.

It was just too good for words. His Bapu had come clear of his tussles with himself. Normally he met him ready with his set questions:

'How is the master? Met him before coming over?'

'Yes.'

'And the maalkin? Met her?'

'Her too.'

'They said anything?'

'No!' He had barked out the 'no!' the first day. But how quickly Bapu's face had fallen! How blank his eyes had gone! The sight of that face had scared him. By and by Bapu had learnt to hide his intense hankering to know the innermost thoughts of the maalik and maalkin. But he didn't want his father's heart broken like the maalik's body.

The next day he had bought a few grams of grapes with his own money and brought them along.

Bapu had broken into smiles. Snatching the bag from his hand he had said, 'Must be from the maalkin!'

He had stayed silent. Bapu was eating each grape as though the elixir of life lay stored in it.

This blissful chewing had stung him deep, deep. His Bapu, to be so swept away by scraps from the haveli? He had blotted out the sight and killed the moment. That very instant. He had broken the bond between Bapu and the haveli. In a taut voice, he had said, 'I have brought them—for you.'

The feeling of freedom Bapu had in the hospital, freedom no wider than the width of the bed, and the tender, soft undercurrent between him and Bapu—he wanted to preserve these. Preserve their warmth in the space between his palms, no matter if his palms got scorched.

Bapu was in comfort here. He was at ease except for the hours of pain. Food came in time, there was leisure and gossip. And amidst fellow patients there was the standing come to him from his age. By the evening he had a bagful of news which he was eager to lay out before him like a banquet the moment he came in.

How liberated Bapu was, away from the haveli! Skidding on the black slime by the well he had indeed skidded far—skidded into the vortex of the love that throbbed unceasingly in people and relationships, in pains and aches. What a wealth of wonder and zeal he had, what an unremitting flow of joy at seeing new things! And what a variety of expressions he was seeing on Bapu's face, the same face that had looked careworn by the weight of servitude! The sight of the youth in the bed next to his, being fed by his father, made him emotional. He couldn't stop talking about it. The warmth that Bapu got by thus talking about it, which parts of him basked in the warmth—didn't he know all this?

When he reached the hospital he was heavy with words roiling within him. On the right side of his forehead was a swelling. It made his eyes heavy. He could have shrugged if off if he wanted to, but he did not want to.

'What happened?' As soon as Bapu inquired in alarm, he poured it all out. What had transpired between him and Tarun Babu he related, of course. But he also spoke about what had not actually transpired between them.

'Have you any idea why he wanted to take me along as his attendant? To make me look like his dog running along behind him with the golf clubs, while he cut a fine figure swinging his club!'

'What did you tell him?'

'What was there to say? I said the master was lying ill at home, you were lying ill in the hospital, therefore, I wouldn't go.'

'Then?'

'He said there are hundreds of people lying ill in hospital, they don't all die. "Tarun Babu!" I raised my voice. "Say Chhotey Maalik!" he shouted, and threw an ashtray at me.'

'Ahhh … ' Bapu fell into thought. 'Did the maalkin say anything?'

'Nothing. She signed to me to go away from there.'

'Why do you bandy words with him? Just tell me this!'

'Bandy words with him? Well, I haven't so far but I will now! Give it back to him so hot that … '

'No, no,' he went pleading. 'You know well enough that the maalkin and maalik both steer clear of him. What chance do you have?'

'I know they steer clear of him, they *can*.'

Bapu's face darkened with abject, craven fear. 'No, no, son. My whole life I have slogged for them, haven't thought twice about it, and now in my old age … '

'You've slogged all your life, but I … '

Bapu lost control, suddenly. An insane excitement drove him. 'Yes, Kishna, you. What do I matter? But you matter, Kishna, you matter. Go wherever you like, get away from here, I will not stop you. I'll not fault you in any way. Make your getaway, go, I pledge my word, go anywhere. If it is a job you have to do, do it anywhere, take it with eyes open, with full understanding of what it implies. Go, go to the village, go to your *tau*. Never mind he is a bad sort, he's our kin. Even if he kicks us dead he'll also stack our corpses in the shade. You cannot bear all that I have borne. My heart is of harsher metal. It bore your mother's death, bore your being roped and tethered. No, no. Don't think, Kishna. Go, run away, right away from this very spot here … '

He wasn't himself. Frenzy swept over him

'Hush, hush, that'll do, Bapu.' He trembled. 'Where will I go? Is it pots of money I have? How will I go? And go leaving you! You couldn't cut your bonds with your maalik all your life and you ask me to cut my bonds with you, my father? Leave my father in this condition? Do you think I'm so low-down, such a no-good chap?' He left without a glance back.

His son's broken, stifled voice buzzed in his ears the whole evening. A storm brewed in him. All the ease and rest of his days here got wrung out by somebody else's darting fist. His hand went to his forehead again and again, as though the red wound on Kishna's forehead was on his own. His leg was strapped to a stand above. The discomfort of not being able to turn dug into his back. But he was not aware of these discomforts. The coin-sized wound he felt on his forehead throbbed, pulsated.

In his mind is no peace, no calm. It is yoked to the haveli, yoked to Kishna, to Tarun Babu, to the maalkin, the maalik. Each face, each scene, is clearly visible to him as he lies stretched out here in the hospital. Who behaves how with whom, who beats, who takes the beating. He knows the shade and colour of everyone's blood out there, knows every fibre of it. Even the walls of the haveli talk to him. There's nothing to look forward to from there now. Only bricks, assaults. The plaster's peeling off the walls. Everything will come crashing down. And the crash will bury Kishna, only Kishna. For he has kept him tied to the stake there. And he himself is lying here, in the care and comfort of the hospital, warming his senile old bones eating, yapping. And out there he, Kishna, is bearing their barbs. Groans rise from within him, strike against the walls of his chest and rebound, drumming.

There's no knowing when he'll be out of bed. And when out, will he be able to function the way he did? If not, who will bear his burden? And there are the flames of the fire leaping in the haveli: who will burn in it, who will escape—there is no definite telling. He himself will be helpless, powerless, mutely watch from his bed the wounds on Kishna's forehead. Why don't you go away, Kishna, why don't you run away? You can't leave me, you say … Yes, how can you leave me …

But I can leave you. I can go away. I can, Kishna. No joking. I can go without fret or fear, gladly. Go in peace. Cut the cord from this end or that, what's the difference? The weave breaks from either end. No, Kishna, no, this is no death, this is release. If I go all the coils will uncoil, the knots un-knot. An unholy chain will break.

He considers the situation calmly—what was possible, lying tied here? Phenyle? Knife? The nerves of the neck? Or of the wrists? He'll see. At the moment it's Kishna he has to think of.

A wave of excitement courses through him. He will be able to do *something.* He will be able to give Kishna his future. He has not done anything for him. Neither seen to him, nor nursed him, nor caressed him nor dressed him. The luckless boy has grown up hankering for his father who was busy slaving for the maalik. Also, quite honestly, what does he have to give his son? Himself, and the history of his slavery written in the reek of his sweat. Which of these two things is he to give? Neither. But there is a third thing. You won't call it suicide, will you, son? No, you won't. The sin of this killing will not taint me. No, it won't. You will understand. Definitely you will understand. My heart is overflowing with love for you, brimming over and overflowing. If I was truly lacking in attachment and love and care …

He was at ease. The more he thought about it, the more his ease spread. Neither fear nor fever, nor fret, nor anxiety remained. He wasn't so bereft of choice as he'd thought. He was doing something, something, whatever it was.

His mind was light, had become tender, expectant. When Kishna came, bearing the wound on his forehead, his resolves strengthened.

'Come over here, here,' he gazed at him with hungry eyes. He made him sit on the cot beside him. He stroked him, and lay back, his hand entwined with his son's.

Kishna was beyond these dialogues of touch and feel. He said, 'Bapu, the maalkin called me last night. Talked with me long.'

But he was not listening. Just looking at him. He wanted to break out crying. He wanted to hold him against his breast and, enfolding him, call upon his own death. If he died thus, bearing his love with him in both hands, he'd be reborn within his son in the next life, and in all lives, he would be deathless.

'Aren't you listening, Bapu?'

'What were you saying? That the maalkin … What was the maalkin saying?'

He was astonished. Where had disappeared the Bapu who sat bolt upright at the very mention of the haveli? Where? The thoughts he'd been thinking all along his walk to the hospital! How new those thoughts were! Of the sort that could bring tears to Bapu's eyes.

'The maalkin said, "Tarun Babu did wrong. He hit you. He's stupid, mindless. He'll improve, become all right. If he doesn't … well, everybody is not fortunate like your father. You are wise and understanding, Kishna. More than that. You are the oarsman of all of us now, Kishna, of me, the maalik, your father, the house." She said she was aware of everything, understood everything. She'd sent the *munshi* to pay my college fees. Also put in an application for some days' leave of absence for me. She was saying she had full trust in me, that she trusted me more than Tarun Babu. Why aren't you listening, Bapu?' He lost his temper.

'I am listening. Listening only to you, Kishna.'

'The maalkin said she had infinite trust in me. More even than in Tarun Babu. After you, she had trust only in me, she said. Only in me.'

'What do you feel?'

'What can I feel. Good thing she trusts me. But I tell you, Bapu, I'm not one any more to fall for sweet words and tender sentiments. She is tying me, as she tied you. I will not be tied. I'm here in this place because of you. I'll stay just till you get well. I'll do whatever you tell me to, live whatever way you keep me. But get this clear, Bapu. I am not leaving you to that tyrant. I'll go, taking you with me. So far you've kept me tied, now I'm going to keep you tied. I'll never untie you. You'll come, Bapu? You've never listened to anything I've said, Bapu, never given me that pleasure. But this time … this time … '

He placed Kishna's hand on his breast. His lips quivered. And from the corners of his closed eyes the waters flowed, flowed—flowed like a river in flood.

seven

The Same Jungle Again

There's a telegram from home. 'Come at once. Urgent.'

What did 'urgent' mean? Any idea or sense of 'urgent' had long since been dead within her, felled by the darts of life. The untoward encountered time and again becomes a bore.

She has not the slightest desire to go. What can it be—a boil come up on *Bhabhi*'s back? Or Bhaijee swept anew by the wish-cum-nerve to take Bhabhi along on his tours? Or perhaps a grand party was in the making. Or Minna was ill. Whatever it was, her lone, single woman's life was a handy nail to which any and every out-of-the-way happening could be hooked. Reflections of this kind sweep through her each time the wind blows from the direction of home.

In the evening she booked a call on Mrs Bhatnagar's phone. She put her purse on the table in front, making it clear that she would pay. Actually, Mrs Bhatnagar oughtn't to be in need of such assurances. She'd given proof time and again. Even if her job added up to just seven hundred measly rupees a month, her standing as a solvent woman had rung out all those times she'd given proof, rung with the ring of pride.

Bhaijee spoke from the other side. 'I can't talk freely on the phone. You come over. Everything is better said face to face.'

What was 'everything?' Whatever it was or was not, Gagan was sure to feature in it.

'They've put me on invigilation duty,' she hedged.

'Let them ask somebody else. You come over without delay. Let us know your date and time of arrival.' He rang off.

For her, Gagan was not a person. He was a setting, a setting that enveloped her from all sides. He was a ready answer to the question-laden emptiness of her life. Bhaijee was avid to convert this ready answer, this available solution, to the fait accompli of 'home'.

But the bare sound of the word 'home' makes thorns sprout from each pore of her body.

Past midnight. The plaintive yelps of dogs rise and fade. The hard thumps of the *chowkidar*'s lathi rap out 'beware!' The hush of night. And she, waiting, slumped on her cot. Waiting. Waiting on and on. Many, many times does she slip out from under the sheet to stoke the hearth with fresh coals. And each time the wavering red tongues threaten to die out again.

When he comes he doesn't knock. He assaults the door. The least delay and he rains kicks and blows upon it. 'Open up fast!'

Tonight is one of the nights he's found his way back home, even if soused and reeling. Some nights he turns up alone, some nights with a couple of cronies, their eyes smouldering in the dead of night.

'Bring out the food!'

The very food to warm which she had spent hours keeping the fire going, now glowers at her. Six plus two: *atta* just enough for eight roties, and here are these three hulks.

'There'll be a slight delay. I didn't know … ' She quickly shakes out the atta into the platter and sinks her hand into it

'Couldn't keep the roties ready?'

'They're ready. But there're these others who've come … '

'When have I come alone?' He aims a kick at her and misses. Pure chance. Now it's not just her body that trembles, but the numerous teachings of Amma setting up tremors within her.

She shuts the kitchen door. Need the others know? What happens between them is to be between them only. Right there in the front room they are, those two. Look at that one, flopped on her bed, dangling a leg. How obscene he looks. She'll change the sheet when she goes in to sleep.

Why should he have blown his top when she swung the door ajar? Need the kicks and thwacks she gets become a public show? And is it anyway only on the body that kicks land?

'I'll soon take care of you.' He grabbed the back of her neck as she sat bent over the flour, and shoved her forward. An inch more and her face would have scorched in the red embers. Sheer luck that she wasn't sitting on the plank. She'd just squatted, half drowsy with sleep, to knead the flour.

'Cooked meat?'

'It's Tuesday today.' And she thanked her stars it was a Tuesday. With the four eight-anna coins tucked into her *pallu* she couldn't possibly have laid out any smacking meal of meat.

'So what it's a Tuesday?' There's no answer to this 'so what?' His eyes are bloodshot already. She trots out Amma as excuse. 'Amma wouldn't have allowed it.'

'And who says it's Amma's raj here?'

She is silent, and her silence stokes his fury. 'Tongue clams shut before Amma, eh? Wags only at me? Couldn't tell Amma?'

'How was I to know there'd be others?'

'Why didn't you know? Don't you see every day with your eyes? Donkeys foraging in your brain? Let me set it right, here ... ' Another blow, and pain lashes at her below the hips.

For a fleeting second she thinks of telling him to bear in mind at least the life growing in her belly, if not her. But this kind of gentle persuasion seems as idiotic as Mother's teachings of abject husband-worship. How could warmth and affection ever flow down the pathways of such teachings? All those nights when she was not cocooned in the warm embrace of love but wrung between the fangs of brute, violent ownership—all those nights lie sucking at her mind like leeches. How many times had she thought: for whom will this family tree bear fruit? For what kind of people? Once she had got hold of pills and swallowed them too, but nothing happened. Why?

The rotis bake. The reek of egg, onion and garlic stirs awake the nausea in her. As the egg pulp begins to set on the bed of onions in the frying pan, he—this caveman called 'husband'—breaks off a piece and shoves it into his mouth. Not once, but again, and again a third time. How is she to tell him that his licking and slurping would finish the whole plateful? She gives a few light turns to the pulp. Then she swiftly brings the pan down, and covers it with a lid.

God knows how many pits they have inside them to fill. They eat non-stop. Eat and burp. Every few minutes they go into raptures at their own prowess in splitting open a whole onion by squelching it between the palms.

Amma gets up once to go to the toilet, peers in and goes back to sleep on her bed in the courtyard. Tidying up in the kitchen, she hopes the slobs would clear off now that they'd had their fill. But they don't. The whole lot's flopped round in the room. Husband on the rug, Debu on the sofa and Jaggi snoring on her bed. The light blazes away.

Outside, the three o' clock buzzer goes off. She stands at the doorway, gazing at the scene in the room. Shocked. Disgusted

Where is she to sleep now? On mother-in-law's bed? With that heavy, flabby body by her side what space would she be left with? Silently she pulls out the mat from under her bed, and stretches out beside Amma's bed. The floor is hard and frozen. The draught from beneath the curtain cuts into her straight and sharp. The mat is prickly, and hurts: compounded by the pain of her own weight, of the child within her, of flinty nails scratching the walls of her mind.

God knows what Mother had thought! Fallen for their sweet-talk, she had, obviously. Never once did she stop to think why, why on earth they were so cheerfully accepting a girl like her with no looks and no college degree. She tries to cover herself with her shawl, tries to arch her body and draw herself close. But her knees refuse to rise over her pregnant belly and make contact with her chin.

Nothing that had happened all these years, no part of it, was her doing. With her small kerchief of pride and courage, she'd kept covering her bloodied body. But what had come of it? Between her mother and them, no bridge of wealth was possible, and it remained not possible. First they asked for a motorcycle, then for a steel cupboard, and then cash for meeting losses in business.

She did want to tell her husband that his business was going to the dogs because of his own ineptitude. But to tell *him*, a base being like him! Helpless, she sought relief in the shade given by her father's death.

'With the breadwinner gone what can a family do?'

Her husband wasn't moved. A day came when he brought over a stranger. And to this stranger, all too obviously, it wasn't roties he was going to serve …

That was her last day there.

It was half past two in the night. From behind the sack of wheat she drew out the money she'd stashed there. And then she stepped out.

She thought once of waking his mother. As a fellow woman she had her streak of kindness, was as repulsed by her son's debaucheries as herself. But then, within her also sat an ever-asking, parasitic beggar woman who knew only the art of putting out her hand.

'Why didn't you think before the marriage?' One day she did ask, driven to it.

'How were we to know that paupers lived in mansions?' Mother-in-law's retort came pat.

Mansions? She fell silent. Even mansions of bare lime and plaster like theirs didn't come up because the lime and plaster wanted to, but because there was a man around with the means to buy the lime and plaster. And the means went when the man went. And it was no small feat of her Mother's that she had given her children schooling beyond bare literacy, that she had provided them cover behind the high, bare walls of heritage.

She never went back. She came to her brother's and stayed put. And gave birth as she had to. Neither attachment nor detachment stirred within her when the child came. She felt only an inert terror.

Soma Bhabhi put the child into her hands. She felt she was not being given a live child, but an object. Whether she had or did not have the freedom to return this object she was definitely moved by a strong desire to assume this freedom for herself.

Just once she took a full look at the moist, pink mass of flesh from which rose the stench of an immoral paternity. Why had she loaded herself with all this, loaded it within herself?

She felt caught in a jungle where lived beings with no future of their own, a jungle in which anyone could keep anyone bonded and bartered.

'Here.' Soma Bhabhi's voice brought her back to earth.

'Lay her next to me.'

For the first time she realised how indifferent one could be even to the feel of a baby lying next to the breast. Mind and body fell apart. Without the veins of shade, even a plant that thrives in the sun withers.

When she came away to Jaipur for her Junior School Training, the child became even more of a stranger. It had become the answer to Soma Bhabhi's barren womb, like water filling up empty holes by its natural momentum.

Back after her eleven months' training period, she saw on Soma Bhabhi's face a scared look, a questioning look, a look of faint grudge of her natural rights as the mother of the child. 'Will you be taking away this little one too, Bibi?'

For two days she stayed in a state of intense turmoil. Was the child truly hers? Could the mere tint and tone of blood make it hers?

She searched her heart. Nothing stirred there. An icy coldness lay massed. She tried to think, why not, why ever not, could she reach for the solace proffered by a tender green plant in the desert of her life?

But she left that right to Soma Bhabhi. In the tiny fist of the baby she let stay the folds of Soma Bhabhi's *anchal*, by now become familiar.

Soma Bhabhi breathed a sigh of relief. 'Also, think, Bibi, when you go out to work where'll you be carting this little one?' She paused a moment. 'It's home here, Bibi. Everyone finds shelter here.'

Soma Bhabhi subtly conveyed to her the fact of her homelessness.

'Yes, you're right,' she'd said, holding fast to her detachment. She stopped herself from searching her mind. She turned her back on this whole chapter of her life. She was born to be a giver in this world. How could ties be snapped that never got made? If ever a breath of some feeling had lived in her, it had died long ago.

The child called her '*bua*'. It did so from the beginning. Soma Bhabhi would cuddle the child in her lap as she fed her, and ask, 'Who's nicer? Mama or Bua?'

'Mama,' the child would swing round to Soma Bhabhi. And Soma Bhabhi would glow with elation.

She would, in these moments, scan Soma Bhabhi's face instead of her child's. Scan it for some trace of doubt, guilt, uncertainty. Nothing clouded Soma Bhabhi's limpid face.

And within her, the small but unbearable knot of being unwanted would loosen. Was it any small service of Soma Bhabhi's that she had given the child home, security and her own family name in return for the rights accruing from procreation that she had appropriated from her sister-in-law?

Any mean service that she had by this act pulled out by the roots the family tree of those butchers?

Sometimes, in the dancing pupils of the child clinging to Soma Bhabhi's shoulder she did see another face too. Again, neither revulsion nor attachment woke within her. The same cold non-involvement, as if, whatever had been was best viewed from far, left untouched. She didn't know exactly why she had become immune to the pangs of intimacy, the ties of blood. What had smoked out the reflexes of fondness and attachment?

Her posting was at Modinagar, in the Junior Training School. She was given charge of both the kitchen and the study schedules of the hostel. The hostel matron had some days ago run away with the students' money. They said she had had some kind of affair with the office clerk. But the clerk was very much around yet. When asked, he'd grin, 'If it was money she hungered for, she'd have stuck around.'

In the beginning, things seemed a little out of joint, but they soon straightened out. She felt at one with this place where stretched out rows of dormitories with flickering lights, and windows draped with curtains made of torn sarees. In front lay a big open field, a vast expanse of dry grass. At the back was the school building that seemed more desolate in the evenings after the din of the day. Then she would come alive somewhat to the pencil-thin line that separated independence from solitude. But just come alive, nothing beyond. She stayed balanced for the most part amidst the goings-on around her. Nothing was hidden from the eye—the low-down tricks of the clerks, their back-stabbing jealousies, their thefts of provisions from the kitchen, their tradeoffs and deals over marks with examinees from other centres. But nothing seemed really untoward. Nothing rankled. The innocent respect that she got from the students kept the soil of her mind moist. The itch to seek out kindred spirits for a sense of belonging left her for good in these surroundings.

Sometimes, now and then, when the fluttering curtains of torn sarees parted and gave right of entry to a vague and faceless sadness, she put her transistor on. At full blast, drowning the silence with torrents of sound. She would reflect, maybe she was sad but she also had the zest now to say '*boo*!' to her sadness. She could go to the market. She could eat *chaat* at Ganeshi's pushcart round the corner, free of the fear of accusing eyes. If in the mood she could go to a movie. She could go up to the lady teachers staying in the big room on the first floor, and bask with them in the euphoria of group life. At the very least, the sun under which she breathed was not anyone's exclusively. It was everyone's, and hence hers too.

The last time she was home Gagan had asked her in private, biting his lip, 'Are you turning me down because of the child?'

She sat still. With Soma Bhabhi around could this be any reason? But she didn't open up with him. 'Haven't really thought about it,' she hedged.

But many times, many, many times, she *had* thought of life with Gagan. Gagan—scoffed at in the home of his brother and wife, both younger than him. Bossed over by them, deprived of even bus fare by the third of the month on charges of overspending. On Gagan's face there flickered always the search for a fragment of warmth and intimacy.

Gagan could be a way out if the craving for a home flowed within her with the same primeval force as before. It did not. What then was the point of keeping Gagan's hopes alive? What could she possibly do for Gagan or for any human being? God knew where had vanished from within her the simple, womanly yearning that steered thought and mind towards the idea of a home.

She came in response to the telephone call from her brother, unprepared for the demands awaiting her. She was firm. No. She would not sign the court notice for divorce. She would never have come if her brother had told her straight on the phone. How grouchy the principal had been! Even otherwise she gave her no easy time, what with her snide remarks. By her reckoning she was not submissive enough for the kind of job she held. And it was the height of irresponsibility on her part, she said, to ask for leave at examination time, even if it was for just two days.

Bhaijee started at her refusal to sign. Nervously he asked, 'Do you think you'd be going back there, some day or the other?'

'I never even think of it.'

'Then why … I mean it'll be good for you too. Without a divorce your chances with Gagan too … '

'Forget Gagan. I will not sign. I will not set that man there free and gift him the chance to ruin some other woman's life too.'

'Not set him free?' Clouds of dense hatred swirled in Bhaijee's eyes. 'Do you think he's helpless without your permission? Do you know that he's trapped the daughter of a widow? That he's got his fangs into her inheritance?'

'How do you know?'

'Jaggi was here. Asking for your address. I didn't give it.'

'Why my address?'

'The girl was asking for you. She's in the Civil Hospital with terrible injuries. The beast pushed her down the stairs, pregnant with his own child. Jaggi was telling me she had wanted to meet you earlier too.'

'But why me?'

'Without a divorce from you her children stay illegitimate.

Legitimate or illegitimate, what is it to us? But a divorce will help you too.'

She was silent.

'Going there wouldn't be a bad idea either. You'll see things for yourself. Take Gagan with you, if you do go.'

Bhaijee's policy was to see to it that the issue of her marrying Gagan never got wrapped up and put away like a bedroll. He wanted it kept unwrapped and live, as though a fait accompli. If he could, he would simply place two chairs, seat her and Gagan side by side upon them, and pronounce them man and wife.

'You won't sign?' Gagan was shaken. 'You watch out. She'll land up one day at your doorstep if you don't get a divorce.'

'Whether she comes over or not I have no intention of going there.' She saved herself from the snake-heads of memories, memories of the beatings she'd taken … But she also poured cold water on Gagan's hopes that were stirring again. Gagan's face fell. It hurt her, but she stayed distant. Why be kind to a man only to give him the brush-off later?

'Anyway, if you do go, don't go alone. Take somebody, even if it's your brother. Who knows how that vicious lot will behave?' Gagan hid his feelings under the cloak of logic.

'No. I'm not going.' She silenced the two men. But within her, thoughts cantered like wild horses.

How they must have knocked around the poor woman! God knew to what growling, slobbering cronies of his they had served her up! And finally pushed her down the stairs for some cruel joke of a reason …

What would she want to tell her? Want to know from her? Was she fortunate enough to have a bhabhi like Soma Bhabhi, with the same warmth for a child conceived in the pits of misfortune?

A face convulsed by sighs rises before her. Grief burns into her, grief not for herself, but for the one who is unseen, unknown, hurt, who is enemy and friend, both. One with whom she has no connection, but with whom she is not unconnected either. And this connection has grown not just because the unseen and unknown one has taken her place, but because their two bodies are bleeding from the same places and the same wounds.

She calmed down and reflected. What would she do with this right that had come to her, of giving or refusing divorce, a right that she had never sought?

When she took leave of Bhaijee she intended to buy her ticket to Modinagar, ticket back to her desolate lean-to, to confront the raging face of the principal.

But when she came away from the ticket counter, her seat and reservation were for Gorakhpur, the abode of her rival and co-victim.

She wasn't going to tell Gagan. If he had to know, he could ask Bhaijee.

eight

Not Without Reason

'No, I'm not going to my parents.' Deepali spoke in firm, steady tones. 'Why should I ? Will it make my womb flower? It will wither or flower only here, *here*, understand? Or shall I go some other place to make it flower?'

And she gave a low, brazen laugh. She also wanted to say, 'Don't think I'm not up to your dirty tricks. The way you're pushing me to my parents! It stinks!' But she didn't say it.

Sitting in the room opposite, cramming for his departmental examinations, Sudhakar thought, how changed Deepali was. Gone bull-headed, and foul-mouthed. The same Deepali who used to reason: 'Don't raise your voice. Once you shout, your tongue will take over and rip like scissors.'

'Shut your mouth! Witch!' Mother-in-law Hiro Rani flicked the swelling *roti* off the fire with the tongs. Then she threw the tongs at her.

They missed. But they set alight Deepali's anger. She rose, hands upon hips, and stalked up to her mother-in-law. 'I'm telling you, *you* keep *your* mouth shut. Sudhakar's mother you may be, but this house is mine as much as yours. Scheme away all you can but I'm not leaving here. I'll die at your doorstep, and it'll be handcuffs for you.'

In her life Hiro Rani had put hundreds of people in their place. She'd shouted at whom she liked. She'd cooed at and taken under her wings whoever she fancied. A husband she had had, but he just disappeared one fine morning. They found his body floating in the canal.

'Nothing I did! Nothing at all to drive him to this. And he's taken off after planting his seed in me.'

Hiro Rani reminisced, face bland. Then cried: 'Even mother earth has to sprout and green. What's a woman without greening? Just a mass of flesh like a bull. Just a horse on the loose, clattering around.'

She vented her spleen, she frothed, fumed. It might have stilled if Deepali's womb had greened, flowered. Six whole years had passed by. For the first two or three years, Hiro Rani was sporting about it.

'What's the great hurry? Play around, eat, gad about. Save your wedding silks from baby piss and baby shit. Indulge your appetite for preening and dressing up.'

And she'd tell her son, 'Study later, son. Take it easy. If you stuff your head too much, your limbs won't do your bidding.'

Sudhakar would glance at his mother and look away. Every night he passed into the world of madness. Left and right, above and below, he squeezed and pinched and pummeled both his flesh and Deepali's. Whom was he trying to rouse? Himself or Deepali? Who could tell?

The viper of doubt reared up in him.

When the mind was not whole how would it seed, how would it produce …

Similar worries of seeding and producing chased away sleep for Hiro too. Her only son—and the bloodline thinning, fading … Hiro nagged without let-up. 'Not put in a loop or coil, have you? Tell me the truth … '

Deepali shook her head with irritation. 'How many times will you ask me the same question?'

After this it was penance and pilgrimage. The *Durbar* of Nizamuddin *Aulia* today. The *Mazhaar* of the Chishti of Ajmer the next day. The Doorway of the *Baba* of the Miracle Waters, the day after. The *Vaid* of Ninety Winters, the *Mahant* of Hardoi, Nakko *Dai*'s medication, Yunani medicines from across the Jamna, the Ripe Old Woman at the mouth of the lane with six strapping grandsons.

From time to time, Deepali went to her parents' also. She could unwind there, be herself, away from Hiro's nagging.

But nothing happened.

From Kanpur, Bhabhi wrote of a good doctor who'd redeemed hundreds. Deepali got ready to go. With Sudhakar, naturally. It made no sense without him in tow. The tests would be joint, no solo event. If it had been, she'd have sprouted.

Sudhakar dragged his feet. God knew who would be shown up. If he it was to be, his wife would never let him forget it. But his fears proved wrong.

Out of Hiro's earshot, Deepali was all soft, gentle understanding. 'This pain is ours. We are in it together. It'll go if it has to. And is it any great pain? So what if there's no child? Would it be any g-r-e-a-t calamity? '

'What greater calamity could there be? Ma can't take it.'

'If she can't, let her adopt a child for herself.'

'No, that's no way out. Your own is your own. No substitute possible there.'

On return from Kanpur they were calmer. The semen was a bit on the weak side, but not bereft of vigour. Medicines would set it right. The course would last a year.

'Let it last a year. What's a year? We're together for life.' Sudhakar was upbeat, all commiseration and sweet reasonableness. Deepali was with him every inch of the way.

When she saw them back, Hiro's face paled, coloured, paled again. What news had they brought? What was in store for her? She hovered around, circling, backing off, circling in again.

Deepali wouldn't finish opening the bedroll. She said nothing. Hiro collared Sudhakar on his way across the yard.

'Tell me, why don't you tell me? What did the doctor say?'

'He's given medicines.'

'For whom?'

Sudhakar paused a moment. And then he said, face lowered, 'For her.'

In a rush of fury, Deepali tightened the straps of the bedroll she was to loosen, and sent it spinning. On angry, stomping feet she came out to the yard. But he scurried for cover in its recesses, the big brave male. He hid, just hid. 'Go on, hide,' she ground her teeth. 'But for me you've always been naked, and you'll remain naked.'

'Why have you done this? Why did you lie?' She sprang at Sudhakar the moment they were alone.

'I know very well what's to be said.'

'Even if it is a lie?'

'Yes, even if it is a lie. I am the man of the house here.'

'Man?' Deepali's face twisted, stayed twisted. Sudhakar flinched. His face whitened, as if the blood had been sucked out by a syringe.

She broke at the sight. A minute ago she was scorching flame. Now she was rippling water.

'Listen! It is just an ailment. Like so many other ailments. You have to face it like an ailment. Simply letting your mind go under is no way.'

Sudhakar tried to stay calm, rational. But the effort hurt, made him mute.

His muteness roused Deepali to anger again. She wanted to tear it from the roots that very minute. If he went dead within, what good were medicines? All right, then. She'd rein in her tongue.

'What are you thinking?' She began again, soft, gentle.

'Nothing. All I wanted was to explain to you that it was the best thing to say to Ma. In your interest ... '

'What do you mean, "my interest"? She's going to chew me up live, the *thakurain*.'

Sudhakar changed tack cleverly. 'How come you call Maa thakurain today?'

'What else is she? Bullying and aggressive and throwing her weight around, like a thakurain. Won't let a fly settle on her nose. Even if God wanted to put a mole on the tip of her nose she'd pluck it off. But forget all that.' She went plaintive. 'You shouldn't have lied about me.'

'What's said is said. Let things go on this way for a while. The period of the injections would be over soon.'

Deepali resigned herself to her fate. Her feet were in mud. Whichever way she turned the mud would squelch and smear her. And if she simply went along with him, there would be odium, stigma, the stigma of childlessness.

Why was childlessness a stigma? If the vine didn't grow, it didn't. It just meant that the roots had dried. Like the roots of countless other things. Why was a man so hungry for the immortality of his lineage that he could spend his life making placatory gestures to his mortality? Why was he so terrified of not being alive that it made his hunger for being ever alive a matter of prestige? He had to have an heir to manage his assets, he argues! If that was all it was, destitute men should be free of the desire!

What heavy toll would this insatiable hunger of his extort? The bare thought made Deepali shudder. She reached for Sudhakar's hand, clutched it fast.

This uncommon intensity of touch … Sudhakar cowered from it, scared. What did it mean?

Brusquely, he said: 'Listen, Deepali. There's something I have to tell you. It's a little awkward, but I can tell you.'

Deepali looked on at him, face raised, eyes fixed.

Sudhakar freed himself from her hand.

'You desire something from me, don't you? I understand your feeling, but for some time I want to abstain. The doctor hasn't said so, but to hold back and be in control has its own benefit. I'll resume when the injections are over.'

Deepali didn't know whether to laugh or cry. Was this what she sought by impulsively seizing his hand? She was simply groping for an answer to this enigma: this enigma of man's hunger for immortality amidst certain mortality. What was this rope round the waist that stretched from generation to generation? The rope that bred and bound more *thakurs* in thakur homes, more Brahmins in Brahmin homes, more Dalits in Dalit homes—what did it mean?

Wasn't there any code of independence by which a person was sufficient unto himself? A code that had no room for the self or the ego? A code that made man accept the truth that he was dust and unto dust he would return. The Philosophy of the Five Elements had chalked out such a grand design for man's sojourn on earth—Go, then return. Don't attempt to bind or put down roots. Who is brother or kin to the end? Rise from fire, rise again.

She reined in her racing mind, furled in the edges of her unfurling sky.

'You are right. I am with you. Whatever you say, do … '

The effort at curtailment was painful. She went weepy. 'So many precious and beautiful things you've given me. What does it matter if this one thing is not there?'

The weepy voice and the deliberate contraction of the self were not what caught Sudhakar's attention. The coddling in the voice caught it. A strong urge to rest his head on her shoulder and fall asleep on the pliant flesh there overcame him. To reach this nursemaid Deepali that he wanted, he made his body small. Nestling his head deep into her side, he circled her body with his arms.

Deepali had to pat his back, gently, just as she would a hurt child.

She'd just got free after serving breakfast to the family, when her mother-in-law bounced the question at her: 'After how many days do you have your periods?'

In Hiro's hand was a bowl. In the bowl was something. The thick layer of ghee on the thing, whatever it was, made Deepali stare. She thought of the miserly way in which ghee was usually spread on her chapatti.

She was amused. Not sore. The soreness that sprang from great-grandmother, and stretched over to grandmother and mother, had dissolved by the time it reached her. Even stones dissolve in the downpour of aeons.

'It's a cycle of twenty-seven days,' she said, composed.

'Cycle?'

'I mean after twenty-seven days.' To elaborate more she didn't have the urge. She took the bowl and put it on a stool. 'Am I to eat up all of it?'

'Yes! All of it and every day.' Hiro Rani hectored, not coaxed. Ghee in her hand, whiplash in her voice.

'But what is it?'

'Why should it matter to you what it is? Nobody's giving you poison. Pure desi ghee it is. Never seen it probably.'

Deepali nearly exploded with rage. But her rage was to be held in leash, under the circumstances. She would have to show a liking for the treatment, even if it was given under wrong and humiliating assumptions, even if it seemed that she was a spitoon into which thick hot fluids could be poured without a second thought.

This state of affairs was to go on, she realised soon. On the soft, fleshy part of her upper arm they sought to tie the hard black string of a talisman fastened to something like the stone of a fruit.

All her newly stitched blouses with gold borders! Just go down the drain, they would! She objected: 'It's no salwar kurta I wear, amma, that'll hide the string with loose sleeves. These are snug fitting blouses. And the string's on the right arm too. I won't go along with all this.'

'I'll see how you won't go along! The cat's out of the bag, *bahu*! Your defects are there for all to see! You'd better pipe down! A woman's beauty is her womb in flower, not clothes and primping.'

Deepali wanted to fling the nearby brass platter at Hiro's head. But as always this too was helpless anger hissing away within.

'What kind of behaviour is this?' Deepali came down on Sudhakar the moment she stepped into their room at night.

Sudhakar had no answer, but not answering had its own perils. It roused Deepali. And rousing Deepali!?

With a pleasant face he said, 'Just for a few days. And Amma was never nice to you in any case. When has she made you happy?'

Deepali was at a loss for words.

The siege was getting stronger. Sudhakar was cosy in the cover she was giving him. But at what cost to his own self and hers? He was looking for reasons to convert the lie into truth, establish it as truth.

How could his conscience stay alive amidst this falsehood?

Now came a time of pain, just pain. Her mother-in-law's violence Deepali could take. She'd never expected anything else from her. She had tried *seva* too, tried ministering to her mother-in-law. When she'd come in as a new bride, her mind was open, lucent. She was eager to wait on her husband's mother, perform chores at her behest with a smile, earn her love. But that path never opened up.

A solid, bigoted *maleness*—that was Sudhakar's mother. Never having had a man to reason with, bring round with words of gentle and bonding persuasion, what could she know of the grace and giving of femininity? Whether this maleness was cultivated for survival, or because a raw strength was needed to hold her own, Deepali didn't know. When she saw her fierce authoritarianism, desperate to extend its sway over any and every one, not anger but sympathy welled up in her. She forgave her. But forgive Sudhakar?

The long strides he'd taken in such a short while from where he'd started! He seemed to have come to believe that *she* was the 'culprit'!

The very word inflamed Deepali. Even if the fault lay in her, in her body, should she feel shame? Why?

What was there in this situation to feel shame or feel inferior? These were imposed values. Accepted meekly. Continuing to be accepted meekly.

Acceptance brought conveniences, facilities. Name, surname, wealth, heritage, capacity, self, family—everything accrued, fell into your lap, the works.

Who or what was this all-powerful force that snatched from man his right to judge and make his options himself? To date, why had nobody fought for the splendour of a life complete, fully owned? Why had people always sought alibis, facades and cover-ups?

Deepali could see all this. But she did not know how she could convey it to Sudhakar. And then, in the effort to communicate could she forget how vulnerable he was, how slippery and shaky the ground between the truth and his public face?

Sudhakar looked evasive these days. The look of the insecure man, caught in his own trap of keeping up appearances. How watchful he looked, how wary!

Deepali pulled herself together. She had come to this house as Sudhakar's life partner, she reminded herself. So she had to keep his secret. She had to tend to her real pain and his show of pain both together and separately.

A swelling always came up in the place where Sudhakar was given the injection, a stubborn-looking knot. It brought in a nagging pain. The doctor said fomentation would help. When she came in for the night, Deepali always brought along the clothes iron. Hiro was not to know what it was that was to be pressed. Just as she was not to know who it was that was getting the injections. Once, just before they were to retire, Hiro insisted that the potion of ghee and tea-leaves be given to Deepali right then. Sudhakar bent down to his mother's ear. 'Not now, Amma. She has to have her injection first.'

Deepali heard, standing by the water filter. His undertone carried across. Humiliation tore through her. But why, she quizzed herself, fighting for balance. Hadn't this drama been going on for months now?

Sudhakar lay on the bed. Deepali was on the floor. She put in the plug to heat the iron and pressed layers of white, soft cotton. Sudhakar bared his hip, and covered his eyes with a corner of the sheet.

The warmth of the fomentation sent him dozing. Sudhakar—so orderly, so disciplined. She took off the plug and kept sitting on the floor.

Not that there wasn't anything to do. Not even that there was anything special she wanted from Sudhakar. It was just that it was night-time and night had been marked as the hour for all living beings to sleep.

The rules handed to a man! The habits! The trodden paths! The footprints to be followed! How heavy was the pressure of conforming! Was Sudhakar doomed to tow this deadweight of rules? All because by the rules of social categorisation he was a *napunsak*, a non-man? Wasn't there any unknown, unseen and un-trodden trail which would be lit by the mere dream of treading it? A trail that would shake awake the mind frozen by the fear of mortality? If Sudhakar didn't win his liberation, neither would she. She would have to bear a double oppression: from Sudhakar and from Hiro Rani. Oppression had fangs and could bite. Didn't she, Deepali, have some means of her own that gave her the fangs of oppression but not the cruelty to bite with them?

Deepali tried to understand why and how all that had been said in the morning had been said. How and why did the proposition of her going to her parents' rise? Of course, for the past two days or so the desi ghee treatment had been suspended. That made a lot clear. The rest was made clear by Nisha, the bahu next door. Obliquely, through hints.

On Nisha's face the urge to speak up fluttered wildly. But below it swam fear too, making her words float without tether.

'Going home, Bhabhi?'

'No! Who says so?'

'Heard it from *Taai*.'

Hiro allowed herself to be called 'Taai' by Nisha because Nisha's people were also thakurs and zamindars.

Nisha lingered around after tea and the formalities of hospitality.

'I'll stick around till Taai gets back. My maa-in-law has also gone with her to the temple. Thick as thieves the two mothers-in-law have become'.

Deepali laughed. Nisha did not like this breezy manner. She moved up close to Deepali, buzzed around her.

'You don't even ask why I'm telling you all this. Any other woman would pester the life out of me.'

'All right. I'll pester you. Tell me,' Deepali bantered.

Nisha's face went thoughtful, cagey. 'Just came over to meet you. Who knows when we'll meet again. Whether we will at all.'

Now Deepali started. She saw the game. The game was to edge her out and get him married a second time. So, tricking Sudhakar too she was—her mother-in-law. Once the barren bahu was out of the scene she'd go at her son hammer and tongs. But how would Sudhakar deal with her? How would he tell her that …

'Is Sudhakar bovine?' Nisha broke in.

Not 'bovine' but 'a clod' was what Nisha meant, Deepali thought.

Deepali was shaken all right but not shaken out of her wits. Her mother-in-law did not really scare her, whatever she did or didn't. She hadn't confronted her as yet, face to face, but knew she could. What did she stand to lose? The right of mastery? The right of possession? The right to violence? The rights of mastery and violence her mother-in-law could claim by tradition and custom. But the right of possession she, Deepali, had too. As Sudhakar's wife. This right had come to her through marriage. She was no one's slave, bought and bound. The stamps of tradition and history that her mother-in-law wore on her face and person needn't scare her at all, no.

To bear this in mind firmly was enough. If Hiro's tyranny increased, she could take refuge by Sudhakar's side, even if Sudhakar …

As soon as she stepped into the room, Sudhakar brought up the incident of the morning's fracas straightaway. 'Your tongue has really become like scissors now. The way you were talking to Amma in the morning! Just shouting her down! You'll be paid back with compound interest one day … '

Deepali cut him short. 'Did you hear what she called me?'

'She has the right to.'

'You have no objections?'

'Right now … I mean, right now, with these injections going on what difference does it make? This is the only time for you to go to your parents'. Later on you'll be needed unceasingly here.'

The crass, need-based logic maddened Deepali. 'You mean I'm not a woman, but a bin which you fill up with the fodder of your forefather's genes? A thing you can send for and send away with the swing of your own needs?'

'You really are getting foul-mouthed.'

'I'm forced to be that, Sudhakar.'

'You have no patience at all.'

'I?' Deepali fixed her eyes upon his face.

'Haven't I told you that it's just for a few days? Right now, it's convenient. And Amma also wishes it.'

'Listen, Sudhakar. Your line of Ammaji's 'wish' and your 'convenience' I'm just not buying.'

'Why? What's wrong with it?'

'What's wrong with anything or anyone, you never get to see. Tell me, how would you feel if it turned out that the person you loved was not what you thought he was?'

'Are you talking about me?'

A look of utter and total resignation spread over Deepali's face. Even the wish to retaliate didn't form in her. She only felt a neutral, granite-hard distance from everything., Side-tracking his question she said, 'Amma is black and white. Obstinate, but so easy to read. What sledgehammers she has for weapons! How crude and transparent!'

Sudhakar flinched but didn't speak. He kept prodding the form and substance of the words that had rained on him. He didn't turn the words over on their backs, though. He didn't want to know what lay below them—the mire of guilt exposed or just mire.

His silence exploded into her in waves. He was not even making an effort to know what she was saying. He was skirting around. Neither now, nor ever, never, opening up and coming free of himself. For how many years had she been taking in the pus of his maleness? Why? Was it for making more men like him, dishonest, unprincipled and pathetic?

Lost for words, Sudhakar slid up to Deepali and put his arms out to her. He tried to draw her to himself. In spite of his vow of abstinence.

What a very male ploy, she thought. The male, smothering every living thing in the tent of shelter his arms afforded .

Deepali resisted the pull of his arms. Very softly she said, 'Be true to your vow of abstinence, Sudhakar. Do *something* well and fully.

Anything. I'm to leave anyway tomorrow morning. You'll have to go on with your make-believe on your own. I don't know for how long.'

With absolute clarity, Deepali was seeing that like her sudden decision to go, the decision not to come back was also forming in her with swift, sure strides.

nine

Morass

'Less or more, everything of mine is yours too.'

The words leapt into Aartee's mind but didn't take voice, didn't emerge. Throwing such ripe, mellow words in the dry rot of their life together seemed a farce to her, a mockery.

And there was no knowing how Amar would take it. When had he ever taken anything she said in the spirit she said it? Worse, he'd sulk. Brood. Think his wife was killing him with honey in place of poison.

She got to her feet but didn't want to leave the room. Thoughts unspoken, incomplete, knocked around her mind. Hovering by the table, she set to, throwing out the rubbish collected in the drawers. But the feel of hard matter in the hands didn't rise into the sensation of touch. Her mind wouldn't calm down. Was disquiet dogging her heels still, scratching somewhere in the regions of her mind?

Amar by now had propped up the newspaper before his face. A screen, a cover. The cover she had to tear apart. And tell the person sulking behind it to breathe freer, easier. Tell him to snap out of it. That nothing had happened to sink him, make him go under. It wasn't laid down anywhere that life had to function by the diktat of his desires.

'I was saying something', she said, though she'd said nothing at all, nothing. She just wanted to catch his attention.

'If only you'd got the biodata ready, things would have been smoother. It's already four or five days since my talk with Verma Saheb. We are the ones in need, all said and done.'

Amar flung the paper down. 'Nobody's all that much in need. I don't want you dancing attendance on the boss under cover of need. Everyone has needs, everyone has problems.'

'You know that Verma Saheb isn't that kind of man. I've told you so many, many times.'

Verma Saheb was generous. He was protective about his staff. But it was best not to launch into all that again. And as for holding a brief for the sadhu-like pacifism of Verma Saheb, it would be courting disaster. His clean goodwill would be brushed aside as cunningly concealed wolf whistles.

Amar never did understand the binds in which she had to labour too. On one occasion, seeing her chance, she'd told Verma Saheb about a job for her husband. Afterwards she'd also made up for the liberty by taking on more than her normal share of work. An able assistant like her was not easy to get. She coped well with the workload, lightened it. She came on time, drew up the drafts *he* was supposed to, chalked out his plans for him, gave him sane advice. Over and above her own duties she allowed herself to be saddled with work not hers. No, she was not in love with her job, not at all. But how long was she to labour like an ox? Kudos in the office didn't come without bottlenecks elsewhere. The unending tug of war between home and the outside never allowed the money to be just spending money, her pocket money. No, no, she was *not* in love with her job.

When she had decided to take up a job she'd reasoned that army people didn't always get peace postings, seldom had their families with them. It was advisable, therefore, to keep herself involved with some work or the other. And then, in the army, who knew when … But office was blind routine, habit, the drugged ease of basking in stable weather. What medals of gold would she be getting from

Verma Saheb? It was Verma today, it could be a Sharma or an Aggarwal or a Niyogi tomorrow. Then a new routine would start, new plans drawn up. And work, loads and loads of work. After that would come the precious nod of satisfaction from the boss, whoever it was. After that the certificate of trust. And through all this the salary remained the same.

Amar could understand these binds in which she was caught if he wanted to. But he didn't want to. He'd rather mope and wallow in the morass of self-pity.

Yet, in the office these days, she really does hover around Verma Saheb like an invisible shadow of his. The office is her only area of hope and expectation. She's his PA, true. But a lot of impetus and initiative have come to rest in her hands these days. She deputises for him, free of fears that he'd press her for extra gratification. In a corrupt and calculating world this piece of earth round here looks clean and pure. On it, it is enough to be efficient, able and conscientious—the core rules, doubtless, of every office.

What is not in the core rules of any office, however, is the occasional—or, these days, the more than occasional—cups of tea she has with him in the late afternoons. She is careful about no sugar straying into his cup. He is diabetic. Thanks to this inside knowledge, she'd once given him a powder made of *methi* seeds and *jamun* stones, ground by herself. Verma Saheb had taken it with much gratitude.

She'd asked him some five days later, carefully casual. 'Had the paste, sir?'

'Yes. I take it first thing in the morning in case I forget. We call it "*Aartee' churan*".'

'I could make some more, sir.'

'No, leave it to my wife now. She knows too. How much will you take on? Thank you so much.'

The sky seemed to caress her head. The sky never touches the head. But it is always there. Arched. Immanent.

In those dark days when Amar came home wounded from the army, she had been PA to S. K. Mazumdar. He looked and behaved like a true heir of the Raj era. The same image of power he projected—unsmiling face, hierarchy-ridden behaviour. The lines were firm and clear for S. K. You laughed or cried strictly with those of your rank, neither above nor below.

To work with Verma Saheb after S. K. was to step into the realms of human warmth and dignity.

Partly because of Verma Saheb's protective nature, and partly, no doubt, because it must have been buzzing all along in her sub-conscious, she opened up to him one day about Amar's war accident. She told him about the shattering of his dreams dreamt from childhood, of rising up to be brigadier or general. And how soon the dreams shattered—within the twinkling of an eye! A full year hadn't passed since his promotion from second lieutenant to captain, when his leg from the knee down was blown up while patrolling.

'Leg blown up?'

'He stepped on an enemy landmine. His right shin was smashed. Treatment went on for a year and more. The wounds healed, and an artificial limb was fitted. But it's not the pains and wounds of the body that are the problem, sir. They heal. It's the pains and wounds of the mind that are bigger, unhealing.'

'He is alone at home when you come to work?'

'No. His mother is with him and my sister-in-law. My son is also there … '

For the first time she was drawing aside the curtains covering the doors and windows of her home. She didn't know that when you poured out your woes to someone, your voice came out so high, frenzied. That in no time at all, your face convulsed with pain normally kept down.

Verma Saheb was mature, experienced. He changed the drift of their conversation.

'But in such cases isn't a ground posting usually given? In other sections of the army?'

'They gave it all right, but he wouldn't have it. Teaching, staff management, administration … offers came from all sides. But he looked neither left nor right, neither ahead nor behind, simply asked for retirement. Went on and on *and* on about how the lower regions in the army were unthinkable for a man of his qualifications. Wasn't he an alumnus of the National Defence Academy?'

Verma Saheb now looked up, surprised.

'You mean he's been idle since then?'

'No, not idle. But in life when the going becomes downhill it stays so … ' She told him how Amar had primed himself, thumped his own back, bridled the steed of his mind. She told him how, on a friend's advice, he'd put in all his money in a cycle business in the cycle bazaar in Panch Kuian Road. Petrol was getting costlier day by day, he reasoned. The survivor would be the hardy bicycle, the only cheap and self-propelled transport. He put his heart and soul into the work, though depression held him by the neck on certain days.

'I can well understand it. Tough going it must have been.'

'No. It wasn't the work that was tough going. It was pitching camp in the middle of the bazaar, after all the style and polish of army life. The bazaar was a place of zero scruple, zero sense of right and wrong. Everything was weighed on the scales of crass profit. Paint and gloss were freely used to coat old goods. Sleight of hand ruled even for the sales of squeaky springs taken out of old mattresses. His spirits sank. Everything was done in naked view here. Stripped of scruple.'

'He left, then?'

'He didn't leave. Things left, just went. His capital went. A fire broke out one night and all went up in smoke. Short circuit? Arson? Who knew? The shops were stacked high with plastic and rubber anyway. What could have survived? We got the news in the morning. By the time we reached there, it was a black and slimy morass that met our eyes. Maybe the fire brigade reached late. We knew nothing. What could we have done even if we knew?'

Verma Saheb lapsed into silence. Behind such a glowing face—such anguish lay? Such ability stayed astir among such trials? Ability so solid and dependable! Why hadn't he given her a better CR last time?

His silence after her outpour unnerved Aartee. Did she *have* to whip the lid off her basket of woes? You got respect as long as the lid was in place. Blow it, and anyone could take a peek inside, see the mess, hide a smile.

'It's sad, very very sad. I had no idea that … Let me see what I can do.' The comfort given was a speck. But to Aartee it was the sky, the world. She was overcome. But to show she was overcome was not the done thing in these surroundings. 'Excuse me, sir,' she got to her feet. And wresting a kind of permission from him she stumbled out of the room.

In the evening he called her in. He pressed her for Amar's bio-data. 'If the details are there before me, I can put across his case well. I have spoken to Aggarwal, by the way.'

'Aggarwal?' She gasped.

'Managing Director of Sarah Services. My bosom pal. Says so at least … '

Back home she broke the news—to reap bitter taunts. Amar called it trickery by the higher ups. What did she know about things? It was a man's world. Ask *him*, he knew …

After her bath, in the midst of getting dressed for office, she coaxed and cajoled Amar. No matter what he said, she was determined not to let slip this chance. Who knew except her what it had taken to bring about this chance? Was there no way of explaining or conveying this knowing of hers? Was it doomed to remain so?

'I thought I could perhaps take the papers with me if they were ready. A day or two later you could go and see him yourself.'

'I've told you I'm in no hurry. I'm thinking of other things.'

'Other things? What other things?'

'Other things. Now you get ready and go. Seen the time?'

He was right. She was late. She'd come to know in the evening, when she got back.

And what she came to know in the evening was shattering.

'With Bhaijee in Meerut, who is a builder,' Amar said. 'I'm going to work in partnership with Bhaijee. Years of experience he has. So what if we've been a bit distant with each other? You have to make distances go. He's my kin, after all. He'll at least take the trouble to throw my body in the shade under a tree even if he does bump me off.'

'You … you understand the meaning of this?' Aartee sputtered. 'You understand the meaning of anything? My job is here. Am I to leave it? Or trundle back and forth every day? Nothing's going to come of this great idea of yours! You know it yourself! The family will break, not to mention other things. What's intelligent about all this?'

'You mean "intelligent" is only what *you* say?'

'I don't mean that. First let's just try out the ways that *are* opening out … '

'Enough! Stop it now! There's nothing more I want said!'

Afterwards, the same silence, the same face-off, the same bogus look of being busy. Bridges lay broken. But why, why? If she could yield and make way for the other's sense of pride, can't the other too, for hers? At least as a return gesture?

When Amar went to sleep, something got into her and she flipped through sundry papers and files in the house. And what she saw in the drawer struck her dumb. A clean folio of his biodata on top of the retirement papers! Three or four photocopies also alongside, neat and clipped together!

Why hadn't he given them to her? Why the deception? Why the bluff? Hurt ran through her. But so what if she was hurt? What value had ever been there of her hurts? This was the way things were, always would be. She should be used to it by now.

The biodata was carefully composed, very, very carefully composed. Amar had not had the slightest inhibition writing about himself: not the least fear of overstatement, of laying it on thick. All his hobbies from childhood onwards, the contests won, the special skills acquired, the medals and trophies got at the Military Academy—it was all there, detailed accounts of every bit of anything done or got by him, like a garment turned inside out. It wasn't easy, this art of not just projecting yourself in words, but of showcasing yourself, splashing yourself.

Joy bubbled within Aartee now. The biodata was impressive without question. She had no need now to be beholden to anyone. She did not have to sink with gratitude for favours shown. Of course everything could go only so far, even with super biodatas like this one. Still …

After the disarray on the home front, Aartee took to keeping her lips sealed. The problems of home she left behind at its threshold when she set out for office. Ammajee manned the food-making job, looked to Anshu's needs too. But nothing more. She could not, would not, sense that there was a third being in the house too, hungry for her mothering. Her son was now her man. Husband-less all these years, Ammaji had raised in Amar a male idol that was to shoulder all things, never be itself in need of a shoulder to lean on.

Didn't Ammaji really see how heavy his load could be, bearing so many blows of life? When she tried now and then to wake her to it, Ammajee boasted and snapped, 'I do nothing other than what he wants. He doesn't have to leave his room, do you know? Tells me to bring his food in there. Thank god, Anshu is asleep by then. I carry his tray in. He eats sitting in his room, watching TV.'

She could not tell Ammajee, 'What's great about it, Amma? Fobbing him off with these nanny's services? What's great about it? Did you ever try to read his mind? So lost you are in self- admiration telling me about these selfless services you've rendered! At the very least, you could sit with him, or get him to come to you. His heart could lighten a bit, his hours gladden a bit.'

But Amma had stopped being a figure of comfort for god knows how long now. She had found fulfilment in wiping Anshu's mouth, washing Anshu's behind.

Every day, on getting back from office, she'd find Amma all set to push her feet into slippers, not bothering to even change her sari crumpled and stained by day-long wear. From temple to home, from home to temple, the ledger of her life was being filled. Suman, her own daughter, born of her own womb, was just as much beyond her ken. Suman's virginity frightened everyone. Two years younger than Amar, the issue of her marriage had stayed on the backburner for years now, either due to her looks or for lack of them. As an earning member of the household she could well afford to take her own time about marriage. And nobody had the nerve to rag her or gossip about her, showing healthy respect for her blunt tongue and bold-as-brass face. Money could absolve a hundred sins.

The biodata had come to her despite Amar. But she couldn't possibly proxy for him. *He* had to meet Verma Saheb for the essential face-to-face meeting. But he stayed indifferent. Luckily, Verma Saheb himself had broached the subject the evening before. And

Aartee got her chance. Before leaving for work in the morning she alerted him, and dinned it into him: 'Don't back out. Be there before twelve noon. And drop in at my cabin first. This is a must!' She hadn't forgotten that it was also the last day for disposing of the Kishanchand Ramchand file. God knew what was holding it up where.

In the room now are three people. One is seated on the revolving chair. Amar sits facing him. Artee is on the chair alongside Verma Saheb's revolving chair. Amar's entry had been greeted with effusive welcome from Verma Saheb. 'Come in! Do come in! You are most welcome. I've long wanted to meet you. Aartee never tires of talking about you.'

The biodata papers rustled in his hand.

'Your eligibility is beyond question. There oughtn't to be any problem. Corporate companies are always on the look out for an all-rounder like you. Perfect!'

Amar's face reddened as he sat facing him. 'Hardly perfection … What I started I saw sink before my very eyes.'

'Happens sometimes, happens. It's all a question of luck, a question of chance. It's also chance, isn't it, that sometimes you press the right button as you are doing now, and set all the machines whirring?'

He glanced at Aartee at his side, at her face aglow with the hue of her lilac-coloured sari. 'Right, Aartee?' He smiled. She smiled too, as if in agreement.

Amar's lobes reddened. God knew what he read into this exchange. It seemed to him fraught with meaning, loaded. Something had to be there between the two, his thoughts raced. Who did anything for anyone for nothing?

'I'd hate to see you going out of your way for my sake … '

'Now, why would I be doing that? Aggarwal is a close pal of mine. Top man there. And you are no undeserving candidate either. Even without me you'd have made it. It's all chance, as I never tire of saying. Just give me a tinkle in a few days, won't you? Things can slip out of the mind, you know. They won't though, in this instance. Isn't she around, never out of my sight?'

The words thumped into Amar's chest, thumped like the beats of a drum.

Verma Saheb's hand reached for the bell. The peon came. The order was placed. In a short while the tea came in. On the covered tray rested three rose-tinted cups of bone china.

The tea tray infused into Aartee's hands the same energy that it did at home. She ran the spoon briskly in the teapot, poured three cups, and held one out to Amar, still stirring in the milk. 'Help yourself to the sugar.'

'Verma Saheb first,' Amar went formal

'No, no sugar for him. It's bland tea for him always.'

'And for you?'

'For her it's Diehard Dieter's Tea!' Verma Saheb laughed, enjoying his own joke, and gazed at her with teasing tenderness.

They sipped their tea.

'If you folks would only come home some day maybe I could take better care of you. Here it's just tea, this dull, brown liquid. Aartee never tires of holding forth on the titbits you fancy.'

His informality jarred upon Amar. So did the sight of the special bland tea he was sipping, as if it was his own home he was in. And as if he, Amar, had come in as a petitioner, not even as a visitor. A petitioner petitioning for a job, after his own efforts had come to nothing. And he'd not come on his own either. He'd been pushed into coming, pushed by a woman. The best thing for him was to withdraw, clear out when there was time yet. No, nothing. Thank you. Thank you so much, so much.

He suddenly felt that she was trying to read his face. Fathom it, hope already tinged with fear. An all-too-familiar current of futility coursed from her to him, him to her.

'So ... 'Verma Saheb held out his hand, standing up. 'I shall do all I can. Take it from me.' And he shook Amar's hand with warmth, firmness.

Amar shook hands with him too, 'Thank you so much.'

'I'll be back in a minute, sir,' Aartee looked at Verma Saheb, eyes wide and asking.

'Sure, yes. Go ahead and see him off.'

'No, you carry on. I'll be fine.'

Aartee knew that stony voice only too well. She could have stayed back, for the Kishanchand Ramchand file was yet to be disposed of. Before lunch was the time fixed for it. But she stepped out on numb feet. In the corridor she walked ahead. He followed. Aartee pressed the bell for the lift. It came. He left.

Back in the office she was tense, nagged by the remains of a frenzy. In her hands now was the file. Verma lit a cigar, not seeming in any hurry.

'Good man. And how very much concerned you are for him.'

Her heart leapt. But she quashed the impulse for a dialogue. She bent closer over the file, wore on her face a look of stern concentration.

'Of course, it's but natural. I can understand'.

Her silence continued.

He changed the subject. 'The case file must be dispatched today for comment. Delay will mean trouble. The hearing is next week.'

She came back from wherever she'd flown to. And she plunged into the file before her as if disposing of it was the only task in the world.

On her table at the office a message lay for her. The clerk said that the boss had rung twice for her. She was late, she knew, but hadn't wanted it known. Amma was not well today. Suman had a maths test to hold in her class, and couldn't stay. Everything fell to Aartee's lot. It got late, later, still more late.

'Good news for your husband,' Verma Saheb welcomed her, half rising from his chair as soon as she stepped in. 'Congratulations! He should have been here in person to hear the good news.'

She had never before seen him thus. His face was free of the barest hint of power or ego—even sympathy, the breezes of which were ever-flowing in his room and about his person.

She could only stammer, tossed between belief and disbelief. 'Really? So soon? But how?'

'Aggarwal himself called. Normally they don't take in outsiders. I knew it. But he couldn't refuse me, you see. And let me tell you, it's a good post. Branch manager. Within three years or four at the most he'll be … ' Verma Saheb scanned her face. Perhaps he looked for the outbreak of wild elation on it.

But on her face a trembling fought with elation. Could gratitude express itself thus? Verma Saheb hadn't ever seen eyes going moist in the effort to laugh with joy.

'I'm so thankful, sir … ever so thankful … I have no words to … '

'Relax.' Verma Saheb looked away, controlling the extreme affection for her rising within him.

'Sir,' she gasped. 'May I go and phone him? Just now?'

'Perhaps you should wait for the appointment letter?' Her face fell. He at once said, 'Well, go ahead. Tell him, no harm. If it eases things for you, why not, go ahead, by all means go ahead. Ring him from here … '

She sprang to the phone like a bird on the wing. Her hands trembled. 'Hello! Yes, Aartee speaking. From the office. Please, Mrs Tyagi, can you call my husband from upstairs, please? Something important. Yes, I'll hold the line. But I can't hold it too long, you know of course … '

Receiver at the ear, hand clutching it, she explained, 'Won't take a minute, sir. It's just the floor above. A short flight of steps … '

'Take it easy.' He drew the file closer to himself, leaving the field clear for her.

'Listen, Aartee here. Listen, forget about leaving for Meerut today. You were going to, weren't you? Don't go. Something's in the offing here. It's practically there. No, no … yes … I'm speaking from the office. No, from Verma Saheb's room. He sent for me just now. And told me! What? Never mind! What's a reservation slip? Tear it up! You haven't paid yet! Yes, I'm sure. I mean what I'm saying! Try to understand! What? Oh! All right, then. I'm putting the phone down. I said I'm putting the phone down. We'll talk at home … '

She rang off, but her face looked as if a voice had lashed it, a scream had rent it.

'Everything okay? Is he happy? I'm sure he is!'

'Yes, sir. Yes, sir. He's happy. Very happy.' She didn't sit. She walked towards the door.

'Sorry! May I go now, sir? I'll come when you need me.'

'Certainly, certainly. You may of course go now.'

A whole lifetime's wisdom and experience rang in his voice. The corners of his mouth sagged.

He called her later in the afternoon. She was alert and on her toes as always. But her eyes were far away. As if engaged in a strife on another front.

'I must thank you again, sir,' she said, seating herself.

'What do we have on our hands now? Which firm?' He spoke in very professional, clipped tones. It was the only rope he could throw to her to haul her out of herself.

Back home in the evening she found that he'd gone. Gone to Meerut, gone by the afternoon bus. He'd left the key with the neighbour. Suman had opened the door herself, getting back from school.

'What time did he go?'

'Who knows?'

'Has Ramu given in the milk?'

'Who knows?'

'And Amma?'

'Don't know.'

She didn't ask about Anshu. No point in it. And she stopped Suman from making tea for her. 'Not for me.'

'Had it already in the office, I suppose!'

She turned to look at Suman. Had Suman too gone cattty about her, gone wily, like Ammaji, like Amar? Everyone was vicious about her, sly! She thought at first of reasoning with Suman, a working woman like herself. Don't you really see that I have to have a wash first, cook dinner, put Anshu to bed? I have to get the house in order—all inside out now. Can I possibly settle down to tea and stretch my legs?

But she said nothing. Just asked for the strength to gather into her hands the four corners of the house threatening to fly apart. Asked it of herself. Just herself.